FAIRWAY PHENOM

MATT CHRISTOPHER®

FAIRWAY PHENOM

Text by Paul Mantell

LITTLE, BROWN AND COMPANY

New York ∿ Boston ∿ London

Little, Brown and Company

Time Warner Book Group
1271 Avenue of the Americas, New York, NY 10020
Visit our Web site at www.lb-kids.com

www.mattchristopher.com

First Paperback Edition

Matt Christopher® is a registered trademark
of Matt Christopher Royalties, Inc.

Text by Paul Mantell

ISBN 0-316-07551-5 (pb)
LCCN 2002103230

10 9 8 7 6 5 4 3 2

COM-MO

Printed in the United States of America

FAIRWAY PHENOM

Malik Edwards sat on the fire escape, his legs dangling off the edge. Down in the street below, his friends Curtis, Luis, and Sean were playing stickball with some kids from the other side of Fourth Avenue. Manhole covers served as home plate and second base, while first and third were a pair of empty trash cans.

Normally, Malik would have been down there with the others, playing stickball on these last, slow days of summer. He would have been busy having some fun before the reading assignments and homework started to pile up, before the days started getting rainy and cold again. But today, somehow, he just didn't feel like it.

It was hot and muggy, and the air hung over the city like a yellow-brown curtain. Off to the west,

Malik could see high-topped clouds gathering. *Good*, he thought. *A thunderstorm's coming.* It would clear the air out, so folks could breathe easy again.

All summer, Malik and his friends had played stoopball and stickball, shot hoops at the playground, and cooled off in the water jets from the fire hydrants. It had been pretty good, as summers went — although he wished his mother could have afforded to send him to camp. Malik knew a lot of kids who screamed and cried about being sent away for two months, but when they came back, they were always bragging about all the cool stuff they'd done. He wished he could go, just once. He wouldn't scream and cry about it. Green grass and trees, and birds singing all the time . . .

"Yo, Edwards, come on down here and play shortstop!" Luis yelled up to him. "Curtis has to go home and baby-sit his little sister!"

"No, man." Malik waved him off. "Later for that, all right?"

"What's up?" Luis asked. "You sick or something?"

"Nah. Just tired. And it's too hot, anyway."

"Then why you sittin' out there?"

"You know what? You're right," Malik said. "Later, man."

He got up and went inside, into the cool, dark living room. He stood in front of the air conditioner for a couple minutes, so the sweat on his T-shirt would dry out and cool him off. Then, grabbing the remote, he flopped down on the sofa, turned on the TV, and started channel surfing.

This time on a Thursday, there weren't any baseball games on. There was soccer with Spanish narration, but Malik didn't speak Spanish. There was an extreme snowboarding contest. Malik wondered where you could snowboard in August — probably New Zealand or someplace like that. And then there was golf.

Malik had never really watched much golf. It seemed totally lame, watching some fat old guys hitting a white ball into a white sky so the camera couldn't even pick it up until it landed on a grassy green and people clapped politely. Bo-ring.

But something about this broadcast grabbed his attention. The man swinging the clubs wasn't old and fat. He wasn't even white — he was a young

3

African-American guy, just like Malik, swinging his club so hard that the ball rocketed straight into space. Instead of polite clapping, the crowd whooped and yelled like they'd seen something totally incredible. Malik leaned forward on the couch and turned up the volume.

"The number-one golfer in the world is showing once again why he is number one," said the announcer. As the golfer strode down the course, people ran along the sidelines to keep up with him, falling all over themselves as they struggled to take his picture. Young girls held up signs saying "Marry me!" as he passed them. Suddenly, golf seemed a lot more interesting to Malik than it ever had before.

Not that he'd ever played, of course. He lived in Brooklyn, for goodness' sake! How was he going to play golf? Besides, he knew what the other kids would say — the same thing *he'd* say if Curtis or Luis suddenly put on orange pants and a hat with a pom-pom on it and went off with a golf bag over his shoulder.

"Well, Bob," the announcer was saying, "this sure isn't your father's golf game anymore!"

"I'll say," Bob agreed. "With a score of sixty-one today, we have a new record for this golf course. The other players are going to have a rough time catching up."

Sixty-one. Sounded good, Malik thought. He'd heard somewhere that in golf, the lower your score was, the better, since it counted how many times you had to hit the ball to get it in the hole. He also knew there were eighteen holes on a golf course. So let's see . . . sixty-one divided by eighteen . . .

The heat must have been frying Malik's brain, because he couldn't do the math, at least not right then. The leader of the tournament, done with his round for the day, waved to the crowd and smiled before disappearing into the clubhouse.

Malik turned off the TV and got up. Golf, huh? He'd only watched for about ten minutes, but it had actually been kind of cool. . . .

He went down to the street in the elevator, to see if the guys were still playing stickball. They weren't, but Luis was still there, throwing the pink rubber ball at the nearest stoop, then running to catch it, over and over again. "Yo!" Malik hailed him. "Whatcha doing?"

"Nothin'," Luis replied, sounding bored. "Everybody went home. You wanna play stoopball?"

5

"Okay," Malik said.

"I'm up first," Luis said.

"What!?"

"My ball."

"Okay." Malik let Luis get in front of him. Luis threw the ball against the steps, and Malik caught it on the fly. "One out."

Luis whacked the ball down again. This time, he got two bounces out of it before Malik, at the curb, scooped it up. "Man on second," Luis said.

"Hey, Luis," Malik said as Luis wound up again. "You ever watch golf on TV?"

"Yeah, man. I hate that stuff. It's so stupid."

"I don't know. I watched one guy today, and it was kind of cool. He hits it so far — like a mile past all the other guys!"

Luis turned and gave him a look. "Malik, man, don't go weird on me, okay? Golf is for old guys and losers."

"Yeah, I guess." Malik backed up, getting ready for the next bounce of the rubber ball. But his mind was still on the picture of the young guy — the one who looked a little like him, only a lot taller — swinging that club and hitting the ball way out of sight.

6

The rubber ball hit Malik right in the forehead and bounced away. "Ha-ha!" Luis laughed. "Wake up, man! You sleeping? Two–nothing, my favor. Still only one out."

Malik checked for traffic, then trotted across the street to get the ball. When he returned, he tossed it back to Luis. "I don't really feel like playing," he said.

"What's up with you, man?" Luis asked.

"Just tired, I guess. Too hot. And school next week."

"Shut up!" Luis ordered, plopping down on the curb next to Malik. "Don't talk about it. I'm not ready for that stuff."

"Sorry."

"Hey, speaking of shutting up — did you hear Old Man Quigley died?"

"No way!"

"Yep."

Old Man Quigley was otherwise known as the "Shut-Up Man," because he was always yelling at the local boys to shut up whenever they played ball in front of his apartment.

So . . . the old guy had died. Malik had never really known him. He was surprised to find that he felt sad about it.

7

"Yeah," Luis said. "There's a big Dumpster in front of the building now. His family's there, throwing his stuff out. And there's this bag full of golf clubs lying right on top. I guess the old guy played golf when he was younger or something."

Malik jerked to attention. Golf clubs? In the trash? "Did you check them out?" he asked Luis.

"Nah. What, are you kidding?"

"Hey, you want to go over there?" Malik asked, getting to his feet. "Maybe there's some other cool stuff."

"Waste of time. It's all junk. It's like the Shut-Up Man never threw anything out."

That sounded cool to Malik. He liked going through old stuff, even if it was junk. To him, it was like looking at something that came out of a time machine. A piece of the past. Junk that once was new.

"I'm gonna go over there," Malik said. "You can come if you want." He was hoping Luis would turn him down. That way, he could check out those golf clubs in peace.

"Ah, okay," Luis said. He hoisted himself up and followed Malik as they headed for Mr. Quigley's building. "But I'm telling you, it's a total waste of time."

❖   ❖   ❖

The houses on Old Man Quigley's block were mostly apartment buildings, with occasional rows of attached private houses — or at least, they used to be private. These days, there were usually three or four families living in each of them, one family to a floor. Mr. Quigley's house had been one of these. He'd lived on the first floor, with a window facing the tiny front garden and the sidewalk beyond. As long as Malik could remember, Mr. Quigley had been sitting by that window, watching the world go by. Other than "Shut up, you boys!" he'd never heard him say very much.

Malik wondered about Mr. Quigley as they approached the building. Had the old man really played golf? It seemed impossible.

There were the clubs, right on top of the big, full Dumpster that sat out front by the curb. So obviously Luis had not been lying — Mr. Quigley had played golf once. It was hard to imagine. The old Mr. Quigley Malik had known was bent over and walked with a cane all the time.

Malik wanted to check out the clubs more closely, but there was Luis, waiting to make fun of him if he did. He'd call Malik a weirdo and a loser. So instead,

Malik checked out an old, broken radio that would have been cool if it were in one piece. Then he pushed aside a stained tablecloth and some chipped dishes to look at some furniture that had been junky even when it was new. All the stuff of the Shut-Up Man's life, now piled up in a Dumpster.

Malik felt sad again. He wished he could have seen Mr. Quigley swing a golf club, just once. It amazed him that the Shut-Up Man had ever been young. But he knew it was true. Long, long ago, he'd been the same age as Malik!

"Didn't I tell you?" Luis said. "It's all garbage. That guy was crazy. Look at all this stuff he kept!"

Malik found a pair of glasses he'd seen on the old man. One lens was cracked, but Malik kept the glasses, anyway. He stuffed them in the pocket of his baggy shorts — a souvenir to remember Mr. Quigley by. But he didn't take the thing he really wanted — the bag full of golf clubs.

Not right then, anyway.

It was only after supper that Malik returned to the Dumpster. He'd loaded the dishes into the dishwasher and set it going. His mom was watching TV in the living room, resting up after a hard day at the office. She didn't notice when Malik silently slipped out of the apartment.

The sun had set, and the street lights had come on. The sky was dark purple, going to black. Malik had to climb up onto the Dumpster to reach the clubs. He grabbed the shoulder strap on the side of the bag —

"Hey!" someone shouted behind him.

Malik's heart gave one big *thwack* inside his chest. "Huh?"

"What are you doing up there?"

It was a woman's voice. Malik turned to look at her. She was standing in the doorway of Mr. Quigley's building — a tall, slim woman about his mother's age who looked like a younger, pretty version of the Shut-Up Man.

"I was just . . . um . . . looking. . . ." Malik felt totally lame lying about it.

"If you want those clubs, you can have them," the woman said. "They were my dad's, but he won't be needing them anymore."

"You Mr. Quigley's daughter?" Malik asked.

"Yes."

"Sorry about your father."

"Thank you. He'd been very sick for a long time. It's a mercy." She sighed. "Anyway, go on and take the clubs. I'm sure he'd be glad someone wanted them."

Not if he knew who it was, Malik figured. *One of the boys he was always yelling at.* "Thanks," he said.

"They're in terrible shape, I'm afraid," said Mr. Quigley's daughter. "Do you play golf?"

"Um, I played miniature golf once or twice."

She laughed. "Well, you'll find real golf is quite different. Anyway, enjoy them."

"I will. Thanks again." Malik waved as he headed home, the bag of clubs slung over his shoulder. Every few feet, he glanced around nervously to make sure no one was watching.

When he got home, he snuck past the living room and into his own bedroom. Shutting the door behind him, he hid the clubs way, way in the back of his closet, behind his winter clothes.

It was the best hiding place he could think of. No one would find them there unless they were looking for them — or unless he was dumb enough to take them out.

2

Malik didn't think about the clubs again till the Tuesday after Labor Day — the day before school started. The time in between was taken up with family visits. First he and his mom went up to the Bronx to visit Uncle Dwight and Aunt Letisha. Then they went over to Ozone Park, way out by Kennedy Airport, to see their Edwards cousins, who lived with their eight kids in a big, old house on a street with giant trees. On Labor Day, Grandma Johnson came over with a ham she'd made, and Malik's little sister, Keisha, pulled the tablecloth and dropped that ham right onto the floor. What a commotion!

So it was only on Tuesday that Malik remembered about the clubs. He was at home, baby-sitting Keisha while his mom was at work. Keisha went down for her nap at two o'clock — she was only four and still took naps, thank goodness! By three o'clock, Malik got tired of channel surfing. There was nothing on at three in the afternoon during the week, even with a hundred channels.

Then he thought of the clubs. They were still there in the back of the closet, where he'd stashed them. As he took out the filthy, old canvas bag, he thought he could smell the Shut-Up Man's stink of mothballs and moldiness.

Taking the bag into the living room, Malik drew out a long club. It had a big wooden head and a metal shaft. The wood of the head was splintered and broken where it met the shaft, but it didn't look like it would come clean off anytime soon. Malik took hold of the rotting leather grip at the top of the shaft and felt the weight of the club in his hand. Spotting a crumpled-up piece of paper on the floor, he stood next to it, lined up his shot, and swung.

Crash! Malik ducked and covered his head as shards of glass from the ceiling-lamp globe sprayed all over the place.

Malik cursed himself for being so stupid. Why hadn't he checked first to see that he had a clear shot?

Oh, well, it was too late now. He'd have to clean it up, then figure out some good story to tell his mother, so she wouldn't know about the golf clubs. She might get mad and make him throw them out, and then where would he be?

"Malik?"

Oh, no — now he'd gone and woken up his sister!

"Go back to sleepy-time, Keisha," he called to her.

"What was that noise?" she asked, stifling a yawn as she came to the open doorway. "Oooo . . . you break something?"

"No," Malik lied. "It was just an accident. Nothing happened. Go back to nappy-bye, Keisha."

"Mama's gonna be mad."

"Shush," Malik ordered. "Do what I told you, Keisha, or I'm gonna tell Mama you were bad. I've gotta clean this mess up. You stay out of here, understand?"

He brushed past his sleepy-eyed little sister and made for the hall closet to get a broom and dustpan. He was on his way back when he heard Keisha's scream of pain.

"Mamaaaaaa!!!! I'm bleeding!"

"Rats!" Malik muttered, dropping everything and

15

racing to Keisha, who was standing in the center of the room screaming, her left foot bleeding in two separate places. "Keisha, what did I tell you?"

But she just kept screaming, making him deaf as he carried her to the bathroom and sat her down on the edge of the tub. "Here, let me clean you off."

The cuts weren't too bad, and, luckily, there didn't seem to be any shards of glass in Keisha's foot. Malik cleaned off the wounds, Keisha screaming as he applied the alcohol. Then he bandaged them up and carried Keisha back to bed. He gave her a lollipop to suck on, so she'd quiet down and maybe even go back to sleep.

Malik needed to think. His mom would be back from work soon, and he knew his story was going to have to be extra good this time. Forget about any baby-sitting money she might have given him. No matter what, this was his fault, and he knew his mama would see it that way, too.

Those stupid golf clubs — it was the Shut-Up Man's ghost getting revenge on him, he just knew it! Those clubs had a whammy on them. He told himself he ought to get rid of them before something else bad happened.

But he didn't. Not just then. He decided to stuff them back in their hiding place till later, when he could figure out what to do. Then he went back into the living room and started sweeping up the mess.

His mom returned from work shortly after five. "Mama," Malik said after she'd kissed him hello, "the ceiling lamp broke."

"It did?" she asked, concerned but not angry. "How did that happen?"

"I don't know, Mama. I was just sitting there watching TV, and it went *kapow!,* and there was glass all over the place, and Keisha cut herself —"

"Keisha *what?!*" His mom was off and running now, headed for Keisha's bedroom. "My baby! Are you all right? What happened?"

"Malik broke the light!" Keisha said, ignoring the threatening gestures Malik was making at her from behind their mother's back. "And he was mean to me!"

"Oh, he was, was he?"

"No, Mama!" Malik protested. "She was so tired she doesn't remember. I told her not to come in the living room, but she didn't listen, and —"

17

"Never mind," his mom said, cutting him off. "You were baby-sitting, and your sister's well-being was your responsibility."

"You gonna punish me, Ma?" Malik asked, the corners of his mouth curling down and tears filling his eyes.

His mother sighed. "I want you to tell me the truth, Malik," she said, sitting him down beside her on Keisha's bed. "The whole story."

"Okay, Mama," Malik said. He looked up at her with as much sincerity as he could muster. "See, a big bird flew in the window . . ."

In the end, she only grounded Malik for the rest of the evening. "School's starting tomorrow," she said, "and I'm going to let you start off with a clean slate. But you stay in your room after supper, you hear? Don't you go out in the street to play with the other kids."

Alone in his room, Malik took out the clubs again and examined them more closely. Three of them had those big, wooden heads. They had numbers on the bottom — 1, 3, and 4. Six clubs had flat metal heads and were shorter in length. They were marked

3, 5, 7, 9, PW, and SW. Malik wondered what the initials stood for. Also in the bag was a putter — like they gave you at the miniature-golf course. This one, Malik knew how to use.

Inside the zippered pocket of the old bag were four yellowed, scarred golf balls. Also some wooden toothpick-like thingies, whose purpose Malik couldn't figure out, and a couple of little round disks — purpose also unknown.

Malik took out the balls and lined them up on the floor. He got his plastic cup from the bathroom and put it on the floor, so that the open top faced him. Then he started practicing putting the balls over the worn carpet, to see how many in a row he could make.

This entertained him for about half an hour, but then it got boring. Malik started thinking back to his first swing of the wooden-headed club, the one that had smashed the light. He wondered if it would have been a good shot — if that crumpled-up piece of paper would have flown into the next room. He tried to imagine how far one of these golf balls would go if he really hit it with all his might. He thought of the young golfer he'd watched on TV —

number one in the world. Malik remembered how far he'd hit it; how all the people *ooo*ed and *aaah*ed and yelled, marveling at how far the ball went.

Suddenly, Malik felt compelled by some strange, invisible force — he *had* to try it. Right now. *Had* to. He took the wooden club with the number five on its head. He took the two oldest, most cut-up balls he could find, since he fully expected to hit them so far that he'd never find them again. And then he tip-toed across the open doorway of the living room and out the front door of the apartment.

He'd be back in five minutes. His mom would never even know he'd been gone. Nothing to it.

He hit the street and looked both ways to make sure none of his friends were out there. That was the last thing he needed, for them to spot him with a golf club in his hand. He took off down the street, looking for a safe place to hit the ball. He found it after a couple of blocks — an alley with brick walls on either side. Across the street was a blank brick wall. He could hit it down the alley, across the street, and off the wall, with no harm done.

Malik placed a ball on a little patch of dirt and weeds where the concrete of the alley had broken.

He didn't want to break this club — the wooden number one club was already busted. He stepped up to the golf ball and swung as hard as he could.

Whoosh! Malik looked up to see where the ball had gone but couldn't spot it. Then he looked down. There it was, still sitting there! The crack in the ball was smiling up at him, as if to say, "You fool! You missed me completely!"

Malik swung again, even harder. Same result. "Okay," he told himself. "I'm gonna swing easy this time and make sure I really hit it."

And that's just what he did. *Thwack!* He heard that perfect sound, the sweet click of club on ball, and saw the ball shoot down the alley — and smack right into the fender of a truck that happened to pass by just at that moment!

The truck screeched to a halt, and the driver's-side door flew open. "Hey, you!" Malik heard a man's voice bark angrily. "What did you throw at my truck?"

Malik took off like a shot, hopping the fence at the alley's back end and cutting through backyards till he came out on the next block. He kept running until he was sure the truck driver wasn't following him. Then he stopped to catch his breath.

There was a park across the street, almost empty at this hour. Malik strolled over there. He casually dropped the second ball down, looking around to make sure he wasn't being observed. He swung, aiming in a clear direction, where there was nothing but a row of trees to hit. No trouble to get into. None at all.

Except his shot hit one of the trees, and the ball ricocheted toward the sidewalk. It narrowly missed a mother walking her baby down the street in a stroller. "Hey!" the furious woman shouted. "You trying to kill somebody? Help! Police!"

Malik was already semi-out of breath from his first narrow escape. Still, he had to flee again at top speed, lest he get himself arrested. He arrived back home totally winded, but he still had to hold his breath as he tiptoed down the hall to his bedroom. He didn't dare make a sound until the cursed club was back with its brothers, safely hidden away.

Man! That Shut-Up Man definitely put the whammy on me! Malik thought. He lay in bed, recovering his breath and wondering where in the world he could safely play golf.

There had to be someplace — but where?

3

Wednesday was the first day of school. There was the usual air of excitement as Malik neared the building. All the kids looked just a little nervous — wondering who would be in their classes, who their teachers would be, and whether they'd be nice.

Kids who hadn't seen each other all summer were sizing each other up. *Who got a hot new look over the summer? Who got braces? Who got zits?* The first day of school could be a really tough day in Sunset Park. If you'd gained a lot of weight, for instance, the kids could be pretty cruel with their comments.

Malik didn't do too badly, considering his voice had started changing. It squeaked once in social studies, and the whole class cracked up on him. But that was the only bad part of the day. His teachers were pretty cool, except for gym. He had friends in his English and science classes. And Mr. Ridley — his teacher for math, which he had last period — was mad cool.

Mr. Ridley had been a minor league baseball pitcher. This Malik already knew from Luis and others, who'd had older brothers or sisters in Ridley's classes. Rumor had it that he threw chalk at kids when they weren't paying attention, but always just missed them, on purpose.

Malik didn't really believe the rumor, but he could seriously picture it happening. Everything about Mr. Ridley was fun and surprising — even the way he taught math.

"So if my dog has six puppies the first year, four the year after that, and seven the third year, should I have gotten her fixed in the first place?" That cracked the class up — they'd been thinking it was a real math problem, because Mr. Ridley seemed so serious when he was saying it. But he told lots of jokes.

And another thing: Mr. Ridley wore a short-sleeved shirt that had a logo reading "Richmond Country Club." Malik knew what that meant — it meant Mr. Ridley was not only a baseball player, he was also a golfer.

The bell rang, and Luis motioned to Malik to come outside with him. Malik did want to hang with Luis, to tell him all about his classes and the kids and the teachers and stuff. But he had to talk to Mr. Ridley first — alone.

"Go on, I'll meet you downstairs in two minutes!" Malik called over the noise of students free for the day and gabbing up a storm.

"By the handball courts," Luis shouted back, then booked it out of there.

Malik waited till the crowd of kids surrounding Mr. Ridley had thinned out before approaching him. "Um, Mr. Ridley, could I ask you a question?"

"Sure," he said. "What's your name again?"

"Malik."

"Malik! That means 'king,' doesn't it?"

"That's right!" Malik said, grinning. "How'd you know that?"

"Oh, I know a lot of stuff," he said. "I'm a math teacher."

"You know about golf?" Malik asked.

Now it was Mr. Ridley's turn to be surprised. "Yes, as a matter of fact, I do. I play just about every week. You?"

Malik paused for a second before answering, "Uh-huh."

"Cool," Mr. Ridley said, nodding. "Where at?"

"Um, I don't really remember the name of the place, actually. It was a long time ago."

"Uh-*huh*. How'd you do?"

"Okay. Um, what do you usually score?"

"Oh, mid-eighties, low nineties. How 'bout you?"

Malik didn't know what to say. Having lied himself into a corner, he now had to pull a number out of thin air. He knew it had to be higher than Mr. Ridley's average — after all, Mr. Ridley played regularly — but not *too* much higher. Malik didn't want to sound like a dork who couldn't swing a club. "Um, about ninety-five," he said.

"Ninety-five's really good for a kid!" Mr. Ridley said, obviously impressed. "For real? Ninety-five?"

Well, now that he was in it this far, Malik had no way to go but forward. "Yup," he said. "Hey, where do you go to play golf around here? I mean, when I played, it was in Florida someplace." He was lying out the wazoo now, but he didn't care. He only wanted to impress Mr. Ridley — and find out where to play.

"I belong to a private club on Staten Island," Mr. Ridley said, pointing to the logo on his shirt. "But there's a driving range by the Sixty-ninth Street Pier."

"No lie?"

"No lie," Mr. Ridley said, chuckling. "There are courses you can get to by subway, too. But take my advice and try the driving range first. You want to be in tip-top form when you hit the first tee."

"Right. I'll do that," Malik said, not quite sure what a tee was, but understanding about the driving range. "Thanks, Mr. Ridley."

"No problem. Pleasure talking to you, Mr. King."

"Mr. King," Malik repeated. "Yeah, I like that. Mr. King."

There were no subways that ran down to the pier at Sixty-ninth Street, but by taking two buses, Malik got to within a few short blocks. He walked the rest of the way to the driving range. As Malik strolled out onto the pier, he could see the island of Manhattan across New York Bay. The sunlight, reflecting off the buildings, made him shade his eyes.

The view didn't stop there. The Statue of Liberty

held up her torch out in the middle of the bay, and to the left rose the Verrazano Narrows Bridge. Once, Malik knew, it had been the longest suspension bridge in the whole world. Till they built some bigger ones. Just as someday there would be new golf champions, even better than the champions of today. Malik could see himself lifting up a big trophy and smiling for the cameras.

The driving range was a series of open booths with green carpeting. Sticking out of the carpeting were little white rubber tubes. People would put their golf balls on top of the tubes, then hit the ball off them, down the pier. But the balls didn't go into the water. There were huge nets strung across the pier, strung on what looked like big telephone poles. The whole pier was covered in green carpeting, and there were little flags with numbers on them to tell you how far you hit your ball.

Malik wondered if people were supposed to bring their own balls. He didn't think so. Most of the people in the booths were hitting balls with a fat red stripe on them. Near the pier entrance was a little shack with a sign that read "Office." Malik walked over and went in.

Inside, an old man with hair growing out of his ears sat on a stool behind the counter, near the cash register. "Yeah? Can I help you, sonny?" he asked Malik in a gruff voice.

"I need some golf balls," Malik said.

The man pointed behind Malik. "See them machines? You put a token in. What size bucket you want?"

"Uh, small, I guess."

"Six dollars," the man said, pushing a button on the cash register. It opened with a ring.

Six bucks! Malik took his money out of his pocket and counted it. There was a five dollar bill he'd saved from last week's allowance, and a lot of loose change. He needed $1.50 to get back by bus — it was an awfully long way to walk — and Malik found that he was exactly one dollar short. "Anything smaller?" he asked the man.

"Smaller?" He laughed, like Malik had just said the stupidest thing he'd ever heard. "Smaller than small?"

"Never mind," Malik said, and left the office empty-handed. He felt like an idiot. Why hadn't he asked Mr. Ridley how much it cost to drive golf balls? And *now* what was he supposed to do? He'd

29

come all the way out here just to hit balls where he wouldn't get in trouble for it, and he couldn't afford even a small bucket!

Then Malik got a bright idea. Some of the booths were empty, and there were a few balls lying not far from the front of each of them. Probably missed shots, Malik figured. Anyway, if he snuck just a little ways out onto the carpet, he figured he could gather enough balls to make his trip worthwhile.

Grabbing an empty bucket, he brought his clubs into a booth and laid them on the ground. Then, making sure nobody nearby was watching, he casually moved toward the front of his booth and stuck his longest club out. *Nothing to it,* he thought happily as he reeled in the nearest ball.

Two others were just beyond reach. He got them by sticking one foot out onto the carpet. No sweat. Now he had three.

Malik looked up at a sign that said "Stay behind yellow line! Danger!" The sign hung just above the yellow line, which ran across the front of all the booths. Looking both ways, Malik stepped over the line, with both feet . . .

There! Quickly, he scarfed up four more balls and

retreated back into the safety of his cubicle. He put a ball on the rubber thingie, reared back, and swung with all his might.

Wham! The ball ricocheted off the side of the cubicle and bounced about ten feet beyond, coming to rest on the carpet with a new smile cut into it by Malik's club.

Undaunted, he put another ball down. This time, he swung even harder and faster — and missed completely. The ball toppled over the edge of the rubber thingie, blown by the wind from Malik's mighty swing.

This was not going too well. Malik changed clubs, selecting one of the shorter, flat-headed ones. He figured he couldn't do any worse. He was right. He did just the same. After six more huge swings, all the balls he'd gathered were gone. Most were just a few feet away on the carpet. The one he'd hit the farthest had rolled along the ground, nestling next to a white flag with the number 50 on it. *Fifty yards or fifty feet?* Malik wondered. He wondered, too, if the white flag was trying to tell him something — like "surrender."

But Malik was not the kind of kid who gave up

easily. Last year, he'd asked this girl he liked to go to the movies with him. She'd refused — not once, but five times — before she finally gave in and went with him, just to keep him from pestering her. On that one date, he'd discovered that he didn't really like her. She had a voice like scratchy nails, and everything she said was stupid.

Anyway, he wasn't about to quit now. He was just getting warmed up. He roved the space behind the cubicles, looking for another empty one with a lot of golf balls within easy reach. He finally settled on one and went to work fishing for balls, edging farther and farther out onto the carpet.

There was a sharp clicking sound, and Malik felt something whiz right by his left ear. "Hey!" yelled an angry man's voice behind him. "Get back behind the line, you idiot! You're gonna get killed like that!"

Malik retreated, but not before grabbing five nearby balls. He had just set one of them on the rubber thingie and was reaching for a club when he felt a tapping on his shoulder.

"Hey!" the same man's voice said, still angry. "You're not supposed to do that, you know — there are balls for sale in the office."

"Oh," said Malik. "Sorry."

The man took the bucket of balls and threw them all out onto the carpet. "You don't go out there and take balls, understand?" he lectured. "If you wanna play, you've gotta buy the balls."

Malik wished he could run away from there, but the man was blocking the back of the cubicle. He had reddish hair and lots of freckles and was wearing a shirt that said "Golf on the Pier." *So he works here!* Malik realized. No wonder he'd taken Malik's bucket!

"So what are you waiting for?" he asked Malik. "Go on and buy some balls, or else go home."

Malik looked down at the ground and sighed. "Don't have enough money," he muttered, almost too softly for the man to hear him. "If I buy a bucket, I can't afford the bus home."

He sighed again, surprised to find that he was close to tears. He'd gone to such lengths just to get here, and now they were chasing him away — him, the potential future champion of golf!

"Hey, kid," the man said, his voice softening. "How much you need?"

"Dollar," Malik said, still mumbling.

The man took out his wallet and held a dollar out to Malik. "Go on, take it." When Malik hesitated, the man grabbed his hand and stuffed the dollar into it. "I said take it. Next time, bring enough money, okay?"

"Thanks," Malik said in a near-whisper. The man made way for him, and Malik went inside to buy some balls.

When he came back, the man was still standing there. "Let's see you swing," he said. "Tee one up."

"Huh?"

"Tee. The rubber thing. Haven't you ever played golf before?"

Malik shook his head.

"Geez, I shoulda guessed, what with those antique clubs. Where'd you get them, anyways?"

"Off the trash."

The man chuckled. "Yeah, I can believe it. Okay, go ahead and swing." He stepped back, and Malik swung so hard he nearly toppled over. The ball dribbled forward and came to rest just beyond the yellow line. Malik wanted to reach for it, but he could feel the man's eyes on him, so he reached into the bucket instead.

"That's right," the man said. "You never cross the yellow line. It's a safety issue, understand? I don't care about the stinkin' balls. It's bad business for me if my customers start getting their heads cracked open. Okay, so swing again — a half swing this time, okay? And slower. Much slower."

Malik did as he was told, although he hated to waste a golf ball on a measly half swing. But to his astonishment, the ball screamed into the air, way beyond anything he'd ever hit — and landed near the blue flag with 150 on it!

"Whoa!" Malik gasped. "How'd I do that?"

"Golf's not about how hard you swing," the man said, chuckling. "It's a finesse game, mostly. Later, when your swing is right, you can swing a little harder — but not much. The idea is to have your swing under control at all times, see?"

Malik nodded, not sure he understood but grateful to the man for any pointers he was willing to give. After all, thanks to him, Malik had just hit his first really good golf shot.

Under the man's watchful eye, Malik hit the rest of the balls in his bucket, using one club after another, swinging slow and easy. Half his shots went far and straight, like that first good one. The others either tailed away to the right or popped straight up or were grounders. After each bad shot, the man would say something:

"Keep your head down!"

"Follow through!"

"You're standing too close to the ball!"

Malik could see there was a lot to learn about golf. He thought of those golfers he'd seen on TV. Man, they were really amazing — 'cause this game was *hard!*

"Mister . . . ?" Malik said when he'd emptied the bucket.

"Call me Al," the man said, extending his hand. "Al Sheinman. What's your name, kid?"

"Malik Edwards."

"Where do you live, Malik?"

"Sunset Park, over by Fourth Avenue."

"Well, you've got a nice, natural swing. You could be good someday, you keep playing."

"You know anyplace to play around here?" Malik asked. "I mean, like, a real golf course?"

"Sure," Sheinman said. "Dyker Beach, over by Fort Hamilton and the bridge. You can get there by subway — the RR line. It's a nice course, but busy. And you'd better call up first and find out how much it is, before you drag those crusty old clubs all the way there from Sunset Park."

"Dyker Beach, huh? Thanks!"

"You come here a few more times first, kid," Sheinman advised him. "Get your swing squared away. Then you go play a round of golf."

"Okay. Thanks, Mr. Sheinman."

"Al, kid. Call me Al. Nice meeting you — and remember, never, ever cross the yellow line."

Malik promised he wouldn't. But as for coming back here before he played some real golf, there was no way. He'd hit some fantastic shots, hadn't he? His swing was good enough right now, Malik decided. First chance he got, he was going to head out to Dyker Beach and *get down!*

4

Keisha, stop crying — I'm on the phone. Can't you see?"

It was Friday afternoon, and Malik was missing a big softball game going on in the park. He'd begged his mother to get somebody else to do the job. But no — she was not about to spend good money when she could get Malik to baby-sit. As Malik had once put it in a moment of rare sarcasm, "Why run when you have a son?"

So here he was, baby-sitting his little sister while all the other guys were out having fun. And on top of everything, Keisha was throwing one of her tantrums. "I want chocolate ice cream!" she shrieked over and over again. It didn't matter how many times Malik told her there wasn't any, that there was only maple walnut. "Chocolate! Chocolate!" she kept repeating at the top of her little lungs.

Malik kept offering her other kinds of treats, hoping she'd calm down, but nothing seemed to work. He was losing patience now. He'd been trying to find out how much golf cost at Dyker Beach. First he'd called information, but he'd gotten the number wrong because Keisha was bellowing so loudly. So he'd had to call a second time. Now he was listening to a taped message on Dyker's phone line telling him how much it cost and lots of other stuff he couldn't hear over the racket his sister was making.

"I said shut up!" he finally exploded. *Weird,* he thought. *I sound just like old Mr. Quigley used to. . . .*

Keisha, terrified, backed away from him, her shrieks fading to quiet whimpers. Malik turned his attention back to the phone. The taped message had gotten to just the part he wanted to hear:

". . . weekdays, twenty-five dollars. Children under the age of sixteen, seven dollars Monday through Thursday, ten dollars Friday through Sunday. Nine-hole children's rate, four dollars Monday through Thursday, seven dollars Friday through Sunday."

There. Ten dollars. That and two rides on the RR subway line came to exactly thirteen dollars. His allowance would just cover it, with enough left over for a cold drink and a candy bar. Man, he thought, his mom really should give him more if she expected him to baby-sit. It wasn't fair — especially not with a kid like Keisha!

The kitchen door banged open and Luis barged in. "Yo! We won, homey! Seven–three! We kicked booty! I hit a triple!"

"All right!" Malik said, high-fiving his friend, then sighing sadly. "Wish I could have been there."

"You *should* have been there!" Luis said, oblivious to Malik's sadness. "It was outrageous. We're gonna do it again tomorrow. You wanna come?"

"Tomorrow?" *That was when he was going golfing!* "Um, I think I've gotta do something tomorrow. You're not playing Sunday?"

"I don't know, man. Can't you get out of whatever you're doing? We need you — they're bringing in some ringer from Park Slope to pitch for them."

"Yeah, but like I said . . ."

"Well, what's so important?" Luis wanted to know. "Your mother making you do stuff?"

"Uh, yeah, that's right," Malik lied. "You know how she is." He felt bad, blaming it on her — but not *that* bad. She'd made him miss today's game, hadn't she? She deserved it. And anyway, he couldn't tell Luis the real reason. Luis would tell everybody, and they'd laugh him clear out of Brooklyn.

He could have canned his plans to go to Dyker, but he didn't. He'd been thinking about playing golf all week, and he was determined to go — softball or no softball.

The next morning, Malik waited till after breakfast to make his getaway. Telling his mom he was going to play softball (even bringing his mitt along for effect), he got his clubs out of the closet and snuck them down the hall.

The worst thing would have been if Keisha had seen him. Of course, she'd immediately say something stupid like, "What are you doing with that bag of sticks?" And his mother would hear, and she'd put two and two together about the light globe he'd broken. She'd take his clubs away, and that would be the end of golf for him, forever.

But Keisha, luckily, was watching Saturday morning

cartoons on television. Translation: She was totally hypnotized. She never even saw Malik walk past her to the front door.

Ten minutes later, he was riding the RR toward Eighty-sixth Street, his clubs clattering in the bag as the train rocked back and forth. He caught passengers looking at him, and he wondered what they were thinking. "Wow, he's a real golfer!" or "Who does that punk kid think he is, with his budget golf bag and those beat-up clubs?" Malik tried to look cool, like he did this every weekend, but he wasn't sure he was pulling it off.

He got off at Eighty-sixth Street and walked the four blocks to Dyker, past luncheonettes and gas stations, grocery stores and delis — typical Brooklyn street life. Then, all of a sudden, there it was. Big, old trees lining a high chain-link fence . . . an old red-brick building with a circular cobblestone drive leading to it . . . a real golf course, right here in Brooklyn!

He walked into the building, fishing his ten dollars out of his pocket, and went up to the booth. "One," he said to the lady on the other side of the glass.

"Name?"

"Edwards. Malik Edwards."

The lady looked at a list she had in front of her. "You have an appointment?" she asked.

"Appointment?"

"You need an appointment. Especially on weekends."

"Huh?"

The lady sighed, exasperated. "Look, read this," she said, shoving a brochure under the glass partition. "You want me to put you on the waiting list?"

"How long is the wait?"

"At least three hours. No guarantees."

"Dang!" Malik shook his head and slowly walked away, devastated. What was he supposed to do now? He'd already missed the start of the softball game. By the time he got back, it would be over.

That stupid Keisha! he thought. If she hadn't been yelling so loud, he would have heard about the appointment rule on the taped phone message. Now he'd gone and wasted his whole day!

He felt like throwing his crummy old clubs in the garbage, right back where they belonged. Malik stormed out of the building, thinking he would just hop the RR right back home and forget the whole thing.

But he'd gone out the wrong door. Now he was on a flat, flagstoned patio overlooking the course itself. From here, he could see three greens, flags fluttering in the wind where they marked the holes. He could also see all or part of five holes — long strips of closely mown grass stretching away into the distance.

There were golfers everywhere — out on the course, standing by a booth where a man in a green shirt took their tickets, sitting at tables on the patio, eating and drinking.

Malik felt like he was in a trance. It was just like on TV, only real! And he was a part of it, even if he didn't have an appointment. With his bag and his cool attitude, he was sure nobody knew he didn't have an appointment. Hey, even though he was only on the waiting list, he belonged here as much as anybody else. And when they called his name, he'd hand over his ten dollars and step up to the first tee, just like the rest of them!

A man on the hole marked 18 shouted and leapt into the air as his putt went into the hole. Malik remembered the feeling from miniature golf. He couldn't wait three hours just sitting around here — he had to *do* something!

He saw a green just off the patio where there were several little flags. Three or four golfers were putting multiple balls, practicing their shots. Malik took his bag and went over to join them.

He soon found that putting on grass was different from putting on the carpet at mini golf. It didn't have any windmills or waterfalls, but it was better than carpet. The ball went truer, and you had to hit it just right. Malik forgot about the time, and when he next looked at his watch, half an hour had gone by.

He was tired of putting, though. He spent another half hour watching golfers hit their tee shots, like at the driving range, except instead of a square of carpeting, there was a closely mown square of grass. Some of the shots were awesome, just like on TV. Malik watched for a long while before getting bored again.

This was going to drive him insane. How could he possibly wait two more hours?

He couldn't. Malik decided to take a tour of the course from outside the fence. It would give him a chance to see the course before he got to play it. Hoisting his bag over his shoulder, he walked through the building and back out onto Eighty-sixth Street. Then he turned the corner on Twelfth Avenue and headed toward the bay.

On his left was the ninth hole — he could tell by the flag. Across the street, on his right, there was what looked like a college campus. A sign, bordered by beautiful flowers, said "Poly Prep School." Inside the gate were well-kept athletic fields, looking even greener than the golf course. There were red brick school buildings. And now, coming through the gates of the school, were four boys about Malik's age, pulling brand new golf bags on wheeled carts.

The boys were dressed in khaki shorts and polo shirts, and they wore matching green hats with gold lettering that said "Poly." Obviously, they were headed for Dyker. And, of course, they had an appointment. Rich boys like that always had appointments for everything, made for them by their parents, their teachers . . . whomever.

Malik hid behind the trunk of an old tree while the boys passed by, so they wouldn't see him toting his ratty old bag. When they'd turned the corner, he resumed his walk along the fence.

About a hundred yards farther on, he stopped. Someone had made a hole in the fence large enough for Malik to squeeze through. On the other side of the hole was a tee. A sign at the side of it said, "7th hole. 430 yards. Par 4."

There was no one in sight on either side of the fence. Taking a deep breath and making a bold decision, Malik pushed through the gap in the chain link and onto the golf course.

If he'd been rich, Malik reasoned, he wouldn't have had to baby-sit his stupid little sister. He'd have heard the part of the phone message about appointments and he'd be playing right now. It was society's fault, he told himself. Those four boys probably never had to baby-sit or do anything else to earn their allowances. He just bet it was true.

Armed with this reasoning, Malik took out a ball and his longest club — the one with the wooden head and the broken neck and the number one on the bottom. Looking around on the square of mown grass, he saw two white cubes marking the edges of the spot he was supposed to hit from. All around were pieces of the wooden things Malik had found in his golf bag — obviously, these were tees, and worked the same as the rubber ones at the driving range! Pleased with himself for figuring this out, Malik took a tee out of his bag, forced it into the hard ground, and placed the ball on it.

He was ready. He stepped up to the ball, just like that guy Al at the driving range had taught him, and swung — nice and slow and easy. The ball soared high in the air, and landed way out in the middle of the mown area of grass!

"Whoa!" Malik breathed, amazed and pleased. Putting the club back in his bag, he strode off toward his ball, strutting like a world-class golfer.

There were four golfers on the green in front of him, but Malik figured he could hit again safely — he was still plenty far from the hole. As he stepped up to the ball to hit his second shot, another foursome walked onto the tee behind him.

"Hey you!" he heard them shouting at him. "Get off the hole!" He could see them waving at him, obviously angry. But he didn't care. He was almost halfway to the green — he figured if the hole was

430 yards long, he had to be out at least 180. They couldn't catch up to him, and they wouldn't take their shots for fear of hitting him.

Or would they?

Malik hit his second shot — another beauty, except it tailed off to the right and into a sand trap. Malik knew about sand traps from watching golf on TV. They were bad places for a golfer to be. He wondered what club to use to get out of one. . . .

The golfers on the green had already gone by the time Malik got to his ball. The foursome behind him — all big, tall, fat guys who waddled when they walked — were still yelling occasional curses at him. Malik couldn't make out exactly what they were saying, but he got the general idea. If they ever caught up with him, he'd be in big trouble.

Malik hit his sand shot in a hurry, using the shortest club he had — the one that said SW. But he only drove the ball deeper into the sand. Again and again he swung until finally he made contact — and the ball sailed way over the green and into some woods on the far side.

Malik hiked up the steep hill to the green, and then past it into the thick woods. Here, the land sloped sharply downhill to the fence that fronted Twelfth Avenue. There was lots of undergrowth, and Malik considered himself lucky to spot his ball without a difficult search through the brambles.

Except it *wasn't* his ball — it was a brand-new one, much nicer than any of the ones he had. Malik took it and stuffed it in his golf bag, then looked around some more. He spotted another ball behind some weeds, also new, also not his. This ball, too, went into the zippered pocket of his bag.

Within two minutes, Malik had gathered seven balls, most of them as good as new, to add to his collection — and he still hadn't found his own! He wanted to stick around, but he knew if he delayed much longer, the mean foursome behind him would be within range. He might get caught here, in the fenced-in corner of the course, where there was no escape except by leaving his bag behind and scaling the fence in a hurry.

He went back up the steep slope to the green. Just as he was about to crest the top of the hill, he heard their voices from the other side:

"You see that kid anywheres?"

"If I get my hands on him, I'm gonna teach him a lesson he won't forget!"

"Hey, over on the tee — you see a little kid around? He snuck right on the course at the seventh tee!"

"Nope. Didn't see anyone — you guys see anyone?"

"Nope."

"Nah."

Malik waited until all the voices had faded, and then waited some more, until another foursome had played the hole and gone on to the next one. Then he emerged and wandered over to the eighth tee. It was too late to finish playing the seventh hole. Anyway, what was the use? He'd already lost count of all those shots he'd taken out of the sand!

The eighth hole was a short one — 150 yards according to the sign, which also said "Par 3." Malik wondered what par was, as he stared at the foursome on the green ahead of him — too close for Malik to aim a shot at. Alone on the tee, he laid out all his new balls while he waited for a chance to hit. He formed them into a neat triangle, making sure all their brand names faced up at him.

Then he heard voices coming up behind him from the seventh green. Dang! Now he was going to have to wait some more!

"Hey, kid," said one of the men, a bald guy with a big cigar. "How much you want for those balls?"

"These?" Malik asked, pointing to his neat arrangement. He hadn't meant to sell them, but hey, why not? He sure could use the money if he was going to take up golf as a hobby.

"Uh . . ." He didn't have any idea how much to charge, but he decided to go for the gold. If the guy laughed at him, Malik would still have seven fairly new balls. If the guy paid his price, Malik would be rich. "Three dollars."

"For all of them?" the guy asked, raising his eyebrows in surprise.

Instantly, Malik knew he should have asked for more — *much* more. It was too late now, though. "Uh-huh."

"There you go," the guy said, handing him three crumpled bills and scooping up the slightly used golf balls. "You get any more for that price, I'll buy 'em anytime!"

The man shared a laugh with his golfing partners,

and they started taking their tee shots — four beauties, each landing on or near the green. "See ya, kid!" the man said with a wave as he rolled his cart off the tee. "You keep undercutting the competition, and you'll be a CEO someday!"

Malik didn't exactly understand, but he knew what the man meant. He had let himself be swindled — but next time, he'd know better.

5

As soon as the foursome in front of him was off the green, Malik teed up a ball. His shot veered sharply to the right and landed in a patch of woods. Malik only had a couple of balls left, because he'd sold all the ones he'd found. So he had to go look for this one, even though it had a cut nearly halfway across it.

In the woods, he came upon two more new balls. Malik put them in his pocket to sell later. Then he walked straight over to the green. He dropped one of the new balls and putted it into the hole.

Just in time, too. As he picked his ball out of the hole, the foursome behind him stepped up to the tee. "Gotta keep movin'," Malik told himself. "Today's not a day to keep score."

The ninth hole was long, and led back to the

clubhouse. There was a boy sitting by the tee area, selling lemonade from a cooler for fifty cents. He was selling something else, too — *used golf balls!* The hand-lettered sign said "Like New — One Dollar Each."

A dollar each! Malik could hardly believe his eyes — or his luck. He had stumbled upon a gold mine! He would come back here soon and go into business for real.

He finished the ninth with two fantastic shots to the green and a long putt that just missed going in. Just as he finished, the guy by the blackboard blew his whistle and motioned for Malik to come over.

That first mean foursome must have reported him, Malik realized. He ran into the clubhouse before the guy in uniform could come after him.

Looking up at the clock in the clubhouse, Malik saw that he still had at least an hour to wait. He decided to bag the whole thing and go home. He'd seen and done enough for one day. But next time he played golf, he'd call ahead for an appointment. And even before that, he was going to make some money selling used balls — like new — for a dollar apiece!

✿   ✿   ✿

Day one of "Malik, Inc." went *extremely* well. In fact, it was the very next day. Malik arrived at Dyker at precisely 8:10 in the morning, carrying a shoebox instead of his golf bag. No playing today. Malik was all business.

He wore long pants, even though it was about a hundred degrees out. No sense getting all scratched up and bug-bitten. Making sure no one was looking, he snuck through the hole in the fence and ran straight for the nearest patch of woods.

By four o'clock, Malik had twenty dollars in his pocket — in addition to the ten he hadn't spent yesterday. He was rich!

Before he left the course, he stopped by the clubhouse and made an appointment to play the following Wednesday — the soonest he could get. "What time you want?" the lady asked him.

Hmmm. He had school till 3:00. And since he couldn't bring his clubs to school (What was he supposed to do? Hide them in his locker?), he had to stop at home after school to get them.

The lady cleared her throat. "You want an appointment or not?" she asked.

"Oh. Yeah. How about four o'clock?"

"I've got four ten. Name?"

"Edwards." Malik was happy. So what if he didn't get to play all eighteen holes before it got dark? Besides, it was cheaper to play after four o'clock.

He'd hit some fine-looking shots the day before, and Malik was sure he could do even better. After all, he was legitimate now — no more sneaking around trying not to get caught and thrown off the course. "Man, I was totally stressed!" he told himself. Besides, he now had some decent golf balls. *Cool.*

Malik rode the subway home and spent the late afternoon watching TV. It was the end of a golf tournament, featuring Malik's favorite golfer and a kid from Spain going head to head — mano a mano. He smiled, picturing himself as the champ and Luis as the Spanish golfer.

Shee-ya. Right. Like Luis would ever play golf! He wouldn't be caught dead doing it — and if he ever found out what Malik had been up to — ay, caramba!

Malik sighed dreamily. He hadn't felt this happy in years! His mom was out somewhere with Keisha, and he had the whole house to himself.

Hey . . . nobody around? Malik got an idea. Getting up, he went into his closet and took out his clubs. Of course, he didn't dare take another full swing inside the house. Instead, he mimed swinging in slow motion as the players on TV took their shots. When they were on the green, he putted across the carpet and into his cup. "Yes!" he shouted, celebrating along with the champ.

Suddenly, the front door of the apartment opened, and Luis burst into the living room. "Yo, Malik, you wanna — *Whoa . . . what are you doin'? Eeeeeeuw!*"

"Luis!" In a panic, Malik tried to shove the clubs under the couch. Seeing it was too late for that, he straightened up and stood in front of the TV. "I didn't hear you come in, man."

"You took those clubs? I can't believe you! What did I tell you about that?"

"I know, bro, but this lady came out and asked me if I wanted them, and she was Old Man Quigley's daughter, and she was cryin' and all, and I figured I'd make her happy. . . ."

"What a load of baloney," Luis said, snorting. "Mmm, and watchin' golf, too? You are so lame!"

Luis started laughing hysterically, pointing at Malik like he'd caught him with his pants down.

"No, man, it's cool," Malik said, trying to make Luis stop laughing, which he finally did. "Sit down and watch for a while. I'll explain it to you."

"That's okay. I think I'd rather get some of my teeth pulled. You listen to me, Malik — golf is for snobs and rich sissies. You watch it too much, you're gonna turn into one."

"Luis, give it a chance. I'm telling you, man, it's way cool. Just watch for a few minutes. It won't hurt you."

Luis looked at Malik like he was a werewolf or something, but then slowly sat down beside him on the couch.

"Now, see that guy with the red shirt?"

"Yeah?"

"He's the number-two golfer in the world. And he's only twenty years old."

"Yeah? What's his name?"

"Jose. Jose Hernandez."

"Hey! He's Latino?"

"No — but he's from Spain."

"No lie? Hey, that's pretty cool. But how come he's not number one?"

"'Cuz my man is number one," Malik said, kneeling in front of the TV and pointing out his hero.

"That guy?" Luis said, wrinking his nose. "He's too short and scrawny to be good."

"Oh, yeah? He hits the ball farther than anyone. Check it out."

They watched as the two golfers hit their tee shots one after the other. "Hey!" Luis shouted triumphantly. "My guy outhit your guy! You see? I told you he's better!"

"It's only one shot," Malik said, but he didn't push the point. He was more focused on getting Luis interested in golf. "Besides, it's not about how far you hit it, it's about who has the lowest score after eighteen holes."

"Yeah, *now* you say that," Luis said with a knowing smirk. "But you know my man hit it farther — he's number one. If not today, then tomorrow, yo."

"Hey, Luis, you know what? I already played golf."

Luis blinked, then blinked again. "You lie like a rug, man."

"No lie — there's this golf course right in Brooklyn, and I played there. Not only that — you know what else? You can make mad money selling golf balls there!"

"Where I'm gonna get golf balls to sell?" Luis said disbelievingly.

"You find 'em in the woods, and then you sell them for a buck apiece!"

"Get out!"

"Serious."

"Shut up!"

"I mean it. You don't believe me?"

"No, man, I don't believe you. Who would believe that?"

"Come with me and I'll show you."

"I'm not goin' on any golf course, yo. I've got a reputation to protect."

"Who's gonna know?" Malik pointed out. "You see this?" He took the thirty dollars out of his pocket. "Where do you think I got this money?"

Luis jerked his head back in surprise. "For real?"

"I kid you not. I'm only tellin' you 'cause, you know . . . we know each other from back in the day."

"All right! When do we go?"

Now it was Malik's turn to laugh. "I thought you said golf was for snobs and sissies."

"It is, man. We're not talkin' about golf here — we're talking about cash mo-*nay!*"

They slapped five, laughing together. "I'm gonna play on Wednesday after school," Malik said. "You can come with me and hunt for balls to sell. Deal?"

Luis glanced at the TV, where the Spanish golfer was just about to tee off again. "Deal, yo! But if anybody finds out about this, I'm denying everything, understand?"

"Hey," Malik said, putting a hand on his friend's shoulder. "We never even talked about it."

We go in through here," Malik said, holding up the broken fence so Luis could slip through. Then he followed, his golf bag slung over his shoulder.

"So where are all these so-called golf balls?" Luis asked.

"Right in here, and all over. Wherever there's woods along the sides of the holes. When you finish with one area, just go on to the next — only be careful, 'cause there's golf balls shooting all over the place. You don't want to get hit by one, believe me."

"Don't worry — you ever see me play dodgeball?"

"And they might try to chase you if you pick up one of their balls, so don't take anything off the greens or the fairways."

"What's the fairways?"

Malik pointed to the parts of the course that had

been mown short so golf balls would roll freely and be easy to hit. "Those are fairways, man. Don't you know anything?"

Actually, Malik had only learned about fairways the other day, listening to one of the foursomes as they teed up. But he wanted to sound cool in front of Luis, and that meant knowing everything about golf.

"Okay, I'm down with that. But there better be money in this, yo. I don't feel like wasting my whole day on some wussy golf course."

"Sheesh!" Malik said, shaking his head. "You try it once, man. I'm telling you, it's cool. You'd be good at it, too. You're a better athlete than me, even."

"Never happen," Luis assured him. Then, weakening, he said, "Well, maybe. If I make enough ducats."

Malik helped Luis find one ball, then left him there to search for more. He headed back out onto the street, then over to the clubhouse to pay his money and sign in. His appointment was for 4:10 — fifteen minutes from now.

After getting his ticket, he went outside to the starter's blackboard. Malik was afraid the man would recognize him from last weekend and kick him off the course. But the guy didn't blink an eye. He just punched Malik's ticket, looking him over without even a flicker of recognition. He must be used to kids running all over the place, Malik figured. This was Brooklyn, after all.

"You'll play with those three guys over there," the starter said, pointing. Malik walked over to his playing partners, who were introducing themselves to each other.

"I'm Vinnie, and this is Earl," said an enormously fat man, shaking the hand of a tall, young guy with a blond buzz cut. Earl was fat, too, although not so enormous as Vinnie. "We're in sanitation. You?"

"I'm a student over at Brooklyn College," the young man said. "Thurman's the name."

"Okay, Thurman," Vinnie said, and they shook hands all around. Then Vinnie caught sight of Malik.

"Malik," said Malik, offering his hand.

Vinnie stared at it a moment before shaking it. "Vinnie," he said, looking at Malik doubtfully.

"Earl."

"Thurman."

And just like that, it was time to tee off. Vinnie went first and hooked his drive onto the middle of the second fairway. "Fore!" he yelled, to warn the golfers playing that hole. They ducked, and the ball just missed them. "Pulled it," Vinnie grumbled.

Earl bounced a ball down the fairway about a hundred yards, then picked up his tee in disgust. "Picked my head up," he said, shaking his head.

Thurman stepped up to the tee. He measured the ball with his club, holding still and breathless. Then he slowly took the club back, hesitated . . . and smashed the ball so far Malik could barely believe it. "Whoa!" he said. "Nice shot!"

"Healthy young fella," Vinnie said approvingly. "You play for the school team?"

"Yeah," Thurman said, putting his club back in his bag.

"What driver you use?" Earl wanted to know.

Thurman took the club back out to show them. It had a 1 on it, just like Malik's club, but that was about the only resemblance. Thurman's club was new and gleaming, with a big metal head twice the size of the wooden one Malik used.

Malik got up to hit his tee shot. The men kept talking, distracting him. He wondered if they were going to shut up so he could hit, but they didn't. Malik decided to swing anyway. He'd show them he wasn't someone to be ignored just because he was a kid.

He swung so hard he nearly fell down. The wind knocked the ball off the tee. It sat there, wobbling back and forth like it was laughing at him.

"That's one!" Vinnie said, chuckling.

"Oh, boy," Earl said, "it's gonna be a long day."

That made Malik really mad. He teed up again. This time he swung even harder, just to show those guys he could hit the ball a long way. This time, the ball trickled about twenty yards. Malik went back to his bag and slammed his driver back into it.

He was furious! Those guys wouldn't have talked if someone else was hitting. They'd distracted him, gotten him all upset. No wonder he'd messed up!

He walked to his ball and took out the flat metal club marked 5. As Malik prepared to swing, he tried to remember what Al Sheinman had taught him back at the driving range. *Slow and easy.*

Thwack! There went the ball, straight as an arrow.

"Hey, nice shot!" Thurman said, giving him a smile and a thumbs-up.

"Thanks!" Malik said, breaking into a wide grin. He couldn't help feeling pleased. Getting a compliment from a guy who could hit like Thurman made him feel proud. It made him want to keep doing well.

Malik wound up with a six on the first hole, and another six on the second. Thurman got fours on both holes, and Vinnie and Earl both told him, "Nice par." *So that's what par means,* Malik realized. *It's the score you're supposed to get on each hole.* So, he was four over par for the first two holes. Malik made it his goal to go two over par on each hole of the course. Next time out, he'd try to beat that score.

On the third hole, he started messing up, hitting everything to the right. He wound up nearly hitting Vinnie, who was over on the second fairway *again,* looking for *another* stray shot.

"Hey!" Vinnie shouted at him. "How about yelling 'Fore'?"

"Sorry," Malik said. "I didn't realize you were way over there."

He knew that Vinnie and Earl didn't like him, and never would, no matter how well he hit. They didn't like kids on their golf course, he could tell.

On the fourth hole, Malik hit a shot that caused a big, fat piece of turf to come up and land about ten yards in front of him. He walked by it on the way to his ball, and heard Vinnie yelling at him again. "Hey, kid!"

"It's Malik," Malik politely reminded him.

"Yeah, whatever. You gotta replace your divots. Don't you know the rules?"

"Um, what's a divot?"

"That piece of grass you tore up. You gotta put it back. Stamp it down so it can grow again. Otherwise, you spoil the golf course for everybody else."

"Oh," Malik said. "Sorry. I didn't know." He retrieved the piece of turf and did as he was told. He felt stupid for not knowing the rules, but there were so many of them to learn! How was he supposed to know them all right off the bat? There wasn't any rule book or anything, as far as he knew.

Earl took a shot on the eighth hole that sliced to the right and into the woods. Malik heard a yelp from somewhere in the trees. He hoped Earl's ball hadn't hit Luis. He also hoped his friend had the good sense to get out of there, before Earl came looking for his lost ball.

On the ninth hole, Malik hit his best drive of the day — although Thurman's went about twice as far.

Malik didn't care. He was proud of himself. Forgetting a rule he already knew, he walked right by Vinnie's and Earl's balls on the way to his own.

Immediately, he heard Vinnie's bellowing voice. "Hey kid! You don't walk in front of other people's balls! Where's your manners? You wanna get killed by my shot, or what?"

"Sorry," Malik said, retreating back behind Vinnie. "And it's . . . Malik."

"Yeah, whatever." Vinnie took his shot. It hooked to the left and over the chain-link fence onto Twelfth Avenue. Vinnie cursed under his breath. Malik caught the word "kids," and realized that Vinnie blamed *him* for his bad shot.

They played the rest of the ninth hole, and when they reached the clubhouse, Malik heard Vinnie announce, "Well, Thurman, nice playin' with ya. Me and Earl gotta go get our dinners — got the little women at home cookin'. You keep it up. We expect to see you in the pros someday."

"Thanks, fellas," Thurman said, shaking their hands.

Vinnie and Earl didn't say good-bye to Malik. They didn't even look at him. It was like he didn't even exist.

"You gonna play the back nine, Malik?" Thurman asked.

"Yeah."

"Good." He patted Malik on the shoulder. "Hey, you've got a nice swing, you know? I was noticing. Nice and natural. You hit some terrific shots, too."

"Thanks!" Malik said, beaming, as they walked up to the tenth tee. He was relieved that Earl and Vinnie were gone. No more getting yelled at for every little thing. No more feeling like he didn't belong there.

"You know, if you want, I could give you a couple tips to make your swing more consistent," Thurman offered. "But only if you want."

"Sure! Are you kidding?"

"Well, some people get offended when you offer to help them."

"Idiots."

Thurman smiled. He stood beside Malik on the tee, watching as he prepared to swing. "Keep your left elbow stiff when you take your arms back. That's it."

Malik took a practice swing. "It feels weird," he said.

"It looks right, though," Thurman assured him.

"And your swing will be more under control. Also, take it back slower, and pause for a second at the top. Then lead with your hip on the way down — and don't move your head. That's it. You're twisting and untwisting, but you want to stay in balance. Just shift your weight back, then forward. Right. Nice. Now hit one."

Malik did. The ball screamed into the sky, then seemed to lift itself into warp speed. Wow — it was the farthest shot he'd ever hit, by a mile!

"Yeah, you're gonna be a golfer, all right," Thurman said, casually teeing up his own ball, like nothing had happened. But Malik caught a little smile on his face.

For the next five holes, Malik played the best, most consistent golf of his life. He even got his first par — a three on the eleventh hole! Thurman applauded and tipped his cap in tribute.

Along the way, he continued to refine Malik's swing. "It's always got to be under control, see?" he said, demonstrating. "So you could stop it at any point along the way if you wanted to. Don't worry, you don't have to kill the ball — it'll travel far if you hit it on the sweet spot — right in the center of the club face."

"Thurman," Malik said after his partner hit yet another perfect shot, dropping the ball just two or three feet from the flag, "how do you know what club to use?"

"Well, basically, you learn by experience how far you hit each club. A driving range is a good place to figure that out. But the longer the club, and the flatter the club face, the lower and farther it goes."

He put his club back in his brown leather bag and came over to show Malik. "Let's see what you've got here," he said. "These clubs with the wooden heads are called woods. The 'one' is your driver — when you need to hit it really far. It's so flat, you only hit it off a tee, so the ball gets some air.

"The three and five woods are for hitting off grass, or on short holes, if the distance is right. These other clubs are called irons. PW stands for pitching wedge — that's for close-in hitting to the green. SW is sand wedge. You can guess what that's for."

"Holy mackerel!" Malik said, realizing that he'd instinctively pulled out the right club that time he was in the sand trap!

"And by the way," Thurman told him, "don't worry that your clubs are old. They were good clubs once, and they still are. One or two of them need a little repair, that's all. You hit the way you're hitting, you can use any old set of clubs."

Malik couldn't stop grinning.

On the fifteenth hole, Malik found Luis standing near the green, wiping sweat off his forehead. "How's it goin'?" he asked his friend.

"Look at all these!" Luis told him, flashing a grin. At his feet was a shoebox filled to the brim with balls. "I only picked up the good ones — this way I make more money!"

"What did I tell you, man?" Malik told him. "It's a gold mine!"

"Hey, what've you got there?" Thurman asked, coming up to them.

"Wanna buy some balls, mister?" Luis asked. "Like new! Dollar apiece!"

"How many you got?" Thurman wondered.

"Thirty-two," Luis said. "I counted them already."

"It's all right," Malik said. "He's my friend. You can believe him."

"How 'bout I give you twenty bucks for the whole box?" Thurman offered.

Luis's eyes bugged out at the prospect of selling all his balls so fast. But he was a businessman, after all. He quickly hid his excitement. "Twenty-five."

"Okay, sold," Thurman said. Whipping out his wallet, he counted up the money. "Just put them in the big pocket of my bag here."

"Wait till you see Thurman hit the ball," Malik told Luis. "He's awesome."

"Not as good as my man Jose Hernandez," Luis said, cocky.

"Almost," Malik said. "Go on, Thurman, show him."

Thurman did, and Luis whistled long and low. "Man, I gotta try this game," he said under his breath.

Malik smiled slyly, knowing his friend was getting hooked on golf in spite of himself.

Luis walked the rest of the round with the two of them, laughing at the few bad shots Malik hit, silent when he hit a good one. Malik knew Luis's competitive juices were flowing — that his friend couldn't wait to see what he could do with a golf club.

When they finished, Malik totaled up his score. "One ten," he said.

"Hey, not bad," Thurman said. "How long have you been playing?"

"This is my first time, actually."

"No kidding! Well, hey, one ten's great for your first time!"

"Thanks!" Malik felt his face go hot with pride. "What did you get, Thurman?"

"Me? Oh, I got a seventy-nine."

"Whoa!" Luis gasped. "No lie?"

"Yeah, but I've been playing for ten years, guys. And I've had lots of lessons. You keep it up, Malik — pretty soon, you'll break one hundred, you'll see. And Luis — you ought to give it a try, too. You look like you could hit a ball." He gave Malik a sly wink, to show he understood what Malik was trying to accomplish. *Smart guy, that Thurman,* Malik thought.

Malik and Luis said good-bye to Thurman and went into the clubhouse. "So," Malik said. "You wanna make an appointment to play?"

"For when?"

Malik shrugged. "How about tomorrow?"

"Tomorrow?!"

"Yeah. I've got enough money left for one more round before I go ball hunting again."

"What am I supposed to do for clubs, yo?"

"I'll lend you half of mine — but you've gotta have a bag. It's the rule."

"My dad has a bag he uses for fishing rods," Luis said.

"Cool. Bring it. Let's go sign up!"

"Yeah! This is gonna be awesome!"

Malik tried to hide his smile. Was this the same Luis who had made fun of him over the set of golf clubs just yesterday?

7

The only available appointment for the next day was for 4:40. "That's a problem," Malik said. "We won't get eighteen holes in before dark. Maybe we should wait."

"No, man, I wanna play some golf. I been watchin' these dudes play all day, and a lot of them stink, you know what I'm sayin'? I could beat them. I'm tellin' you."

Malik had to laugh. He knew how hard it was to hit a good shot. Luis had not gone to the driving range — ever. In his whole life. He had never hit a golf ball, even in the street! How was he going to beat anybody? Malik worried that Luis would get sick of golf in a hurry, once he realized it wasn't as easy as it looked.

But Luis took Malik's laugh the wrong way. "You think I can't beat you?" he asked, a challenge in his look and tone. "I could beat you. You only played once, and you didn't play that good. Anyway, I'm a better athlete than you. You know it's true, man. You even said so yourself."

It *was* true, so Malik didn't say anything. "Two for tomorrow," he told the lady behind the glass partition. He pushed their money through the hole in the glass.

"Name?"

"Edwards."

"Four-forty," the lady said. "If you're late, you lose your time. There's always people trying to get on the course. Busiest one in the whole country."

All the way home on the train, Luis was bragging — "Aw, man, I'm gonna get a hole in one! And wait till you see how far I hit it!" — and on and on and on.

Malik really wanted to get Luis into golf, so he didn't say anything. But he knew a storm was brewing. The first bad shot Luis hit, there was bound to be trouble.

❖   ❖   ❖

79

"What *is* that thing?" Malik held up the camouflage-patterned, padded fabric shaped like a large, elongated triangle.

"I told you, it's my dad's fishing-rod bag," Luis said. "Now gimme some of your clubs to put in it."

Malik took out the driver, the 5 wood, 3 iron, 7 iron, sand wedge, and the putter. "Here you go," he said. He knew Luis would complain if he didn't give him enough clubs. Besides, Malik figured Luis might as well lug the driver and putter around, carrying all that extra weight!

As they stood to the side of the first tee, next in line to play, Luis could not stand still. "Man, it's already four-forty, and we're just chillin' here!" he complained, hopping from one foot to the other. "It's gonna be dark before we're halfway done!"

"I told you that yesterday," Malik reminded him. "Didn't I say we should wait till next week?"

"You didn't tell me we had to wait around like this. Why don't these guys hurry up?"

"There are slow people playing in front of them. You can't just hit the ball right at them — somebody could get hurt."

Luis had a lot to learn about golf. Malik was more than happy to teach him, showing off all he knew. But he was afraid Luis wouldn't want to hear it from another kid. Luis was used to being the big cheese, the coolest kid on the block. Nobody told him what to do — *ever.*

Finally, it was their turn, and they stepped up to the tee. "Me first!" Luis said, taking out the driver and putting a tee into the ground.

Malik stepped back to watch. Good thing they were playing just the two of them. Malik wondered why that was. Hadn't the lady said there was a waiting list, even at this late hour?

Luis took a mighty swing, and actually hit the ball hard. But his body had been pointing in the wrong direction, and the ball flew off to the right, toward the ninth fairway.

"Fore!" Malik yelled.

"Why you shouting like that?" Luis asked. "That shot was good!"

"Just warning the people to duck." Malik took the driver and stepped up to hit his shot. "Keep an eye on your ball. Sometimes people might pick it up."

Malik's shot was straight down the middle — one of his best shots ever. "Yes!" he hissed, shaking the club back and forth.

Silently steaming that Malik had outhit him, Luis walked off after his ball.

"Careful!" Malik called after him. "Stay out of the way of their shots!" But Luis didn't turn around. He just kept walking.

Since Malik's ball had gone farther, he walked up the fairway until he was parallel to Luis's ball, and waited for him to hit.

Luis's back was to Malik. He took a swing but nothing happened. He took *another* swing. Nothing again — except a big divot that went flying into the air. Then Luis swung a third time, and the ball took off. It hooked through the thin line of trees and onto the first fairway, not far from the green. "Nice shot!" Malik called. Luis waved and put his club back in the fishing-rod bag.

Malik's turn to hit. He was about fifty yards from the green. From the way he'd hit the other day, Malik figured he needed a pitching wedge. But it wasn't in his bag, and Luis was already walking toward the green. Sighing in frustration, Malik took out the next best thing — his sand wedge — and hit it. But he had to swing extra hard to make up for the shorter club, which threw him off, so his shot landed well short of the green. Dang! Why had he given Luis his pitching wedge? Next time, he'd make Luis come over and give him the right club.

Luis's ball was not quite on the green, but he took out the putter anyway. Malik knew you weren't supposed to use a putter if you weren't on the green, but he didn't say anything. He could see that Luis was already ticked off about missing the ball twice in a row.

Luis's putt wound up about ten feet from the hole. He putted again — without waiting for Malik to shoot, which he was supposed to do, but oh, well — and his ball just missed. Then Luis tapped it into the hole. "Five," he said.

Malik was about to hit his shot, but then he stopped, straightening up. "What? You had more than a five, man!"

"Did not."

"Yes, you did. You hit three shots over on that other fairway."

"Those were practice swings, yo."

"You didn't take practice swings any other time," Malik pointed out.

"I did *that* time," Luis said, not backing off.

"Fine," Malik said, shaking his head. "Five. Can I hit now?" He took his shot, but he wasn't really concentrating. The ball sailed way too far, right over the green and into the high grass — called "the rough," because it was rough to hit out of.

Malik hacked at the ball, missing it completely. "That was a practice swing," he told Luis.

"Yeah, right!" Luis said.

Malik took another swing, and this time hit the ball perfectly. It looped into the air, hit the ground only four feet from the hole, and stopped cold. Saying nothing, Malik took the putter out of Luis's hand and putted the ball right into the cup.

"Five," he said.

"You got a six, yo!" Luis said. "That was a shot — you were trying to hit it."

"You got a seven, then," Malik shot back.

"Five!"

"Fine. Two fives, and that's that!" Malik put down two fives on his scorecard — with asterisks next to them. On the bottom of the card, he drew another asterisk, with six and seven next to it — their real scores.

From now on, he was going to watch Luis like a hawk. He knew his friend wanted to beat him in the worst way. Well, if he was going to do it, he'd have to do it honestly.

No way Malik was going to let Luis get away with cheating — unless, of course, he let Malik cheat, too.

Luis had a bad second hole, and an even worse third hole. Malik must have felt sorry for him, because he didn't play too well, either. Better than Luis, though, for sure.

By the fourth hole, Luis was showing his frustration openly. Dribbling his drive just a few feet in front of the tee, he slammed the driver into the ground.

"Hey!" Malik said. "Easy with that club — one of my woods is already half broken from that kind of treatment." He didn't know that was why, but thought it was a good guess.

"I hate these clubs!" Luis complained. "I gotta get me some real clubs, man."

"It's not the clubs," Malik said. "If you want, I could show you —"

"I don't need you to give me lessons," Luis said hotly. "Just hit the ball, okay? Then I'm gonna take a do-over."

"A do-over?" Malik repeated, rolling his eyes. "Okay, whatever."

If Luis was going to play it that way, fine — so would he. From then on, whenever one of them missed badly, they dropped another ball and hit it, not counting the extra stroke. Malik knew this made score-keeping ridiculous. But Luis kept telling him his score after every hole, expecting Malik to write it down like it really counted.

When they finished the ninth hole and stopped for a drink in the clubhouse, Luis said, "Add it up, yo. Who's winning?"

"We're not playing for real," Malik pointed out, but Luis wasn't listening.

"Just tell me the score," he said.

"Okay. I've got a forty-five, and you have a forty-seven."

"Hey, I'm beating you, man!"

"No, Luis — lower is better, remember?"

"Oh. But it's only two strokes, yo. And it's my first time — I'm gonna win by the time we finish."

"If we finish," Malik said. "We'd better get back out there."

"I'm on it," Luis said, tossing his soda can and grabbing his bag. "Let's go."

Malik finished his bottle of water and followed Luis over to the tenth tee. The sky was getting darker, but it wasn't because of the time. Clouds were rolling in fast. Maybe, Malik thought, that was why there hadn't been a waiting line at the first tee — maybe everyone else had heard the weather forecast and stayed away.

"From now on, we play for real, okay?" Malik proposed. "No do-overs. That first nine was just for practice."

"Okay, deal," Luis said. "But I'm keeping score."

"No way."

"You don't like it, we can both keep score."

"Cool." Malik breathed a sigh of relief. This time, there would be no cheating — they'd each be on guard against the other — and it would be a real match between them. Malik had had enough of Luis's bullying. He, Malik, was the more experienced golfer, and he was going to beat Luis fair and square — no matter what.

He hit a tremendous drive, right down the center of the fairway, then stepped off the tee without a word.

Luis took a deep breath, swung, and hit his best shot of the day. It landed right by Malik's ball, then bounced another twenty yards. Luis turned to Malik with a smirk of pride on his face. He, too, said nothing. The match was on.

Responding to the challenge, both boys played their best golf of the day. Malik had to admit that Luis was a fast learner. Oh, sure, his swing was too long and too fast, but he was a good natural athlete, and that made up for a lot. With some lessons, Malik thought, he really could be great.

Man, what he himself wouldn't have given for half a dozen lessons from Thurman — or Al Sheinman at the driving range. Maybe Al would let him help out around the range in exchange for some lessons. . . .

They were tied after the fifteenth hole, when the first clap of thunder sounded.

"Now what do we do?" Malik said. They were as far from the clubhouse as they could be. It would take them a good ten minutes to walk back — maybe five if they ran full speed.

"We play faster," Luis said. "The thunder's still far away. Just hit."

Malik had his doubts. He had seen a news story on TV once about a golfer hit by lightning. The guy was in a coma for a week before he pulled through. The story said golfers were "at risk," because of the metal in their clubs, and that they weren't supposed to hide under a tree, but stop immediately and head for the clubhouse.

"I think we'd better quit," Malik said, hearing another distant rumble of thunder.

"You quit, I win," Luis said.

Malik bit his lip. Luis would tell *everyone* that he'd beaten Malik his first time out on the course. He'd say Malik was a quitter and a chicken.

Malik stepped up to the tee and hit his drive. It duck-hooked off to the left and down a rocky slope. Luis tried to hide his smile of satisfaction as he took the driver out of Malik's hands.

Luis's drive was right down the middle of the fairway. Malik swallowed hard. If Luis beat him on this hole, the sixteenth, he'd have only two holes to make a comeback. And if the thunder got any closer, he might not even get the chance!

His only hope was to tie Luis on this hole. That way, if the storm came, it would be Luis who chickened out and said, "Let's quit now." The match would end in a tie. That would be okay with Malik. He didn't need to win — just to not get beaten.

He walked down the fairway, then cut to the left to find his ball. Luis could see Malik from the center of the fairway, but he couldn't see Malik's ball, which was halfway down the slope, lodged behind a rock.

There was no way Malik could hit it. If he dropped the ball back onto the fairway, he'd have to take a penalty stroke, and Luis would win the hole!

Thunder rumbled, closer now. It was do or die. Malik heard the little voice of temptation in his head. *Go ahead, drop another ball,* it said. *Drop it onto the grass where you have a clear shot to the green, but where Luis can't see you do it.*

Malik felt in his pocket for his spare ball. There it was. A sudden twinge of guilt hit him, and he almost stopped himself. But when he heard Luis yell, "Come on!" he took out the ball and dropped it on an open patch of grass. Then he pulled out his nine iron and hit a perfect shot!

The ball landed on the green, not far from the

hole. "Hey!" Luis shouted in obvious dismay. "Good shot, yo!"

"Thanks," Malik said, his voice humble. He sure hoped Luis wouldn't notice the guilt that had to be written all over his face.

Luis's second shot fell short of the green, and he whacked the ground with his club again. Malik didn't stop him. Luis had a right to be mad — if he knew what had *really* just happened, he'd be furious.

Malik dropped his second putt for a par — four. Luis got a five. The thunder drew closer and closer. "Come on, man, let's quit now!" Malik urged.

"You quit, I win," Luis repeated, stalking off the green and over to the seventeenth tee.

Malik followed, watching the darkening sky and wondering if they were both going to get fried.

They hit their shots quickly. They were the only golfers in sight now. Glancing at his watch, Malik saw that it was nearly eight o'clock. Maybe the darkness was from night falling, he thought hopefully. Maybe the storm would miss them. . . .

They could barely see their tee shots land, and they trotted toward their balls, in a hurry to finish. Malik was off to the left, Luis to the right.

Malik watched as Luis took another huge "practice shot." "That's two!" he shouted.

"No way, man — I was practicing!" came the predictable response. Luis hit again, and this time his ball landed on the green.

"That's three!" Malik yelled, ignoring Luis's cries of protest. Malik hit his shot, and it landed on the edge of the green, close enough to putt. "That's two!" he said, making sure Luis got his meaning.

Each boy holed out in two putts. "I still lead by one," Malik said. "With one hole to go."

"Yeah?" Luis responded, whipping out his own card. "Well, according to my scorecard, I lead you by one."

"How do you figure that?" Malik exploded.

"You cheated on the last hole, that's how. You think I didn't notice you switched balls? I checked it when you took it out of the hole, yo. You think I'm some fool or what?"

The fact that Luis had caught him made Malik even more furious. "Yeah? Well, you took an extra swing on your approach shot *this* hole — and don't say you didn't!"

Luis was about to answer, but there was a huge thunderclap, and both boys jumped with fear. "Yo, let's finish out!" Luis ordered. He hit a quick drive, not a bad one considering, and gave way to Malik.

They played the eighteenth so fast that neither of them hit very well. Malik had trouble counting his own shots, let alone Luis's. They putted out in a hurry as the rain started to fall, then ran to the shelter of the clubhouse, pelted by the sudden downpour. Lightning flashed out of the darkness, lighting up the course behind them.

"Are you kids crazy?!" a maintenance worker shouted at them as they came into the building. "Don't you know you could get killed like that? Next time you hear thunder, you come in right away — you understand?"

Both boys nodded dumbly, then sat down on a bench to catch their breath and count up their scores.

Malik's card was soaked, and some of the numbers had run. He added up his own score, giving himself a seven on the eighteenth. He had a fifty-one for the second nine. Not bad. If he hadn't been rushing through the eighteenth, he could have broken fifty. Now he wished he knew what his true score on the first nine had been. Maybe he would even have broken one hundred for real. Now, he'd never know for sure.

"What'd you get on eighteen?" he asked Luis, dreading the answer.

"I got a six, man," Luis mumbled.

Malik could tell he was lying, even if he didn't know for sure that Luis had taken at *least* seven shots.

"Come on, yo!"

"No, for real," Luis insisted. "What did you get?"

Malik frowned. "Six," he lied, staring Luis right in the face.

"You lie like a rug!" Luis said, giving him a little shove to the shoulder. "Don't cheat, yo! I beat you fair and square!"

"What? No way!" Malik shouted, shoving back.

Before he knew it, the two of them were throwing punches at each other. "Hey, hey, cut it out!" the maintenance man yelled. "None of that in here, or you won't be allowed in anymore!"

Malik and Luis allowed him to pry them apart. "Go on home, now," the man ordered them. "You wanna play golf, you gotta grow up a little."

The rain had almost stopped by the time they

stepped out onto the cobblestone driveway in front of the clubhouse. "I beat you, man," Luis muttered.

"You are such a liar!" Malik shot back. "Give me my clubs back, yo."

"Here," Luis said, removing them from his dad's fishing-rod bag and dropping them on the hard ground. "Take your ratty clubs back. Who wants them, anyway? This game is stupid — just like you!"

"Hey, you dweeb, don't drop my clubs like that!"

"See you in school tomorrow, loser," Luis said, taking off by himself as Malik stooped to pick up his clubs.

"Yeah? Not if I see you first!" he called after his friend — make that *former* friend. *Man! Luis is such a baby*, Malik thought. *Can't stand to lose, even to his friend who had more experience than him.* Luis had ruined a perfectly good day of golf for him, and didn't even care.

Now Malik was holding the 3 wood in his hand — the club with the partially broken neck. Seized by a sudden rage, Malik took the club and walked over to a nearby sycamore tree. With a mighty swing, he wrapped the club around the tree, then threw it as far as he could.

8

The next day, Friday, Malik woke up in a foul mood. His arm hurt above his elbow, probably from hitting the tree so hard with that club. He wished he hadn't done that. What was he thinking? That a new club would just appear in his bag the next day?

But the worst part was the feeling in the pit of his stomach. He and Luis were enemies now. All day today in school, Luis would be telling everyone that Malik played golf — and even worse, that he cheated!

In school, Malik found himself glancing around to see if kids were giving him funny looks. He thought he spotted a few — friends of both him and Luis who were giving him plenty of space. He spaced out through most of science class, busy the whole time coming up with a strategy for dealing with Luis and his lies.

Denying it wouldn't do any good, he knew. So he decided to counterattack.

"Hey, Hector," he said, leaning over to the kid sitting next to him. "Guess what?"

That was how it began, and he kept it up all day, telling everyone he knew what a cheater Luis was. At lunch in the cafeteria, Luis was sitting with a bunch of kids, making them laugh — with a story about Malik, no doubt.

Luis spotted him, then turned away again. He said something to the other kids, and everyone laughed even louder, shooting glances at Malik.

By the end of the school day, Malik had had about all he could stand. Spotting Luis coming out of the building, he went over to him. "Yo!" he called, ready to hash things out.

But Luis was in no mood to talk. "You liar!" he yelled. Dropping his book bag to the ground, he launched himself at Malik, fists flying.

Malik put his arms up in self-defense, then started swinging back. "Yo, cut it out, man! You're the one who's lying about me!"

"Yeah, right," Luis said, still whaling away. "You tellin' everybody I played golf with you and cheated! What's that about?"

"You did! And anyway, you were telling everyone I was the cheater!"

"That's a lie!" Luis roared, launching another round of punches.

"Hey, hey, hey! Cut that out right now, you two!"

Mr. Ridley's voice rose above the din of kids yelling "Fight! Fight!" and cheering on the combatants. The teacher stepped between the two boys, ending the free show. He held Malik by the back of his shirt with one hand and Luis's shirt with the other. "What's going on here? I thought you two were pals."

"He's been talkin' trash about me," Luis claimed. "Lyin' and stuff. Tellin' people I'm a cheat."

"He *is* a cheat," Malik said. "I beat him at golf yesterday, and he lied about his score."

"Golf?" Mr. Ridley said. "Golf is not a contact sport, guys. And if you cheat on your score, you're only cheating yourself."

"I beat him fair and square," Luis said, still hot with anger.

"Did not!" Malik shot back.

"Look," Mr. Ridley said patiently. "I want to talk to both of you in my office, right now — one at a time."

He walked them back inside the building. Malik could hear the kids behind them, talking about them, giggling. He and Luis were now the laughingstocks of the whole school — first of all, for playing golf, second of all, for caring enough about it to fight over it!

"Well, I'm through," Malik told Mr. Ridley while Luis sat and steamed in a chair outside the office. "No more golf for me." It was going to take long enough to live down as it was. The last thing he needed was to keep going out on the course with his ratty set of clubs and no friends to play with — only fat guys with cigars who yelled at him, and fantastic players like Thurman who played better than Malik ever would in his dreams. What was the use of torturing himself?

Mr. Ridley sighed and sat back in his chair, clasping his hands behind his head. "Malik," he said, "I know you're feeling frustrated and disappointed right now — but don't quit playing golf. You liked it right away, didn't you?"

"Yeah . . . I guess."

99

"In fact, you loved it, until you and Luis had a fight about it — until it came between you and your best friend."

Malik sat stone silent, listening.

"You know," Mr. Ridley said, "I've been frustrated by golf plenty of times. Everybody gets that way — it's such a difficult game. But mastering golf is all about mastering your own frustration. You can't hit a good shot if you're angry. Have you noticed?"

Malik had noticed, all right. But he couldn't see himself ever really mastering his frustration.

"Tell me something, Malik," Mr. Ridley said gently. "Why did you invite Luis to play with you?"

"I don't know," Malik said. "I was stupid, I guess."

"No, really — why did you?"

"Because . . . because I liked golf, and I wanted my friend to like it, too."

"Exactly. But what both you and Luis have to understand is, with golf, you're really playing against yourself and against the course. It's true, you can compete against each other, but you're way too new at the game to be doing that — neither of you even has a handicap."

"A handicap?" What was Mr. Ridley talking about? Did you have to limp or be blind to play golf?

"A handicap is an amount you subtract from your score when you're playing against someone, to make the game fairer."

"I don't get it," Malik said.

"Well, say your average score is one hundred, and par for the course is seventy. You'd subtract seventy from one hundred to get your handicap — thirty. And when you play, you'd subtract thirty from your score to get your score with handicap. So if you shot one ten —"

"I'd have an eighty!" Malik said, liking the idea.

"Right. And if Luis had a one twenty, but his handicap was forty-five —"

"He'd have a seventy-five. Wait a minute — that means he'd beat me, even though I played better."

"Right. That's how you do it if you want to compete with each other. And naturally, you can't get a handicap unless you play enough times to create an average score."

"I get it," Malik said. "But Luis isn't ever going to play again, Mr. Ridley. Not with me, anyway."

"We'll see about that," Ridley said. "Go outside, and let me talk to him."

Malik headed home, not waiting for Luis to come out of Mr. Ridley's office. Luis could call him if he wanted to apologize, because Malik sure wasn't going to be the one who blinked first.

But Mr. Ridley had convinced him not to give up on golf. Maybe sometime, he could get one of his other friends to play. Curtis or Hector, maybe. . . .

Meantime, he would keep playing and improve his game. He would be way better than any friend who decided to try playing. That way, there'd be no competition between them. They'd listen to Malik's advice on how to grip the club and swing it. They would understand that, until they got good at the game, he, Malik, was the man.

Too bad about Luis. He and Malik had been best friends since third grade. But oh, well — if Luis was too immature to admit he was wrong, that was too bad. Malik would have to leave him behind, until Luis did some growing up.

❖   ❖   ❖

On Saturday morning, Malik went to the driving range to see if Al Sheinman would give him a lesson in exchange for some work. He was walking down Fourth Avenue, headed toward the bus stop, when he saw something that made him stop short. At first, he thought it was a collection of junk on somebody's front stoop. As he got closer, he realized it wasn't just junk. This was a "garage sale" — and there, on the steps, leaning against the handrail, was a full set of golf clubs!

Not old, crummy ones like the set he'd gotten for free from old Mr. Quigley's daughter. These were really nice clubs. The woods had big metal heads, the kind that all the other golfers at Dyker had. The grips were in good condition. None of the necks were shattered, and the clubs were clean and shiny.

"How much for these?" Malik asked the man who was holding the sale.

"Seventy dollars."

Malik felt his heart sink right into the ground. Seventy dollars was *way* more than he could afford. "Oh. Never mind."

He was about to go when the man said, "Okay, sixty."

"I've only got thirty," Malik explained. "Could you hold them for me till next week? I could have sixty by then."

"Sorry," the man said. "I can't hang onto any of this junk anymore. Today's the day. Sale's over at five o'clock. Look, you got fifty bucks? I could let you have 'em for fifty. By five o'clock, they're gonna be gone at that price, I can tell you for sure."

Malik wanted the set of clubs so badly he could taste it. If only he had fifty dollars! But where could he get his hands on that kind of money?

Then it hit him. He knew exactly how to make some fast cash. "Hey mister — can you hold the clubs till five? I promise to get you your fifty dollars."

The man smiled. "I don't know, son. If I wait till then and you don't show up, I'm stuck with the clubs. And somebody might offer me more than fifty. I'll do my best, though."

"Thanks — I'll be back with the cash. You can count on it!"

Malik turned around and headed for the subway station. Between his allowance, which his mom had given him that morning, and the money left over from last week, he had exactly thirty dollars. All he had to do was make another twenty selling used balls, and he'd have a new set of golf clubs! Well, not exactly new, but compared to his old set, this one might as well be.

Malik arrived at Dyker around eleven A.M. and started looking for balls right away. He carried with him a white plastic shopping bag that he'd found blowing along the sidewalk on this sunny, windy day. The only thing was, there weren't very many balls in the woods, and a lot of those weren't worth selling.

Maybe he and Luis had fished the waters dry in the past week, he thought. He'd never imagined the pickings would be so slim. Well, he consoled himself, he had all day. He could stay here till four-thirty and still be back in time to get those clubs. He only hoped the man would hold them for him, and that nobody would tempt him with a bigger offer.

Noon came. Then one o'clock. He still had only a few good balls to show for his efforts. At three he finally found out why. There, on the fourth tee, stood none other than Luis! His one-time friend was standing above an empty shoebox, counting up a wad of bills, wearing a big smile on his face. Seeing Malik, his smile faded, then returned, even wider than before. "Yo, thanks a lot for the money-making tip, fool," he said, then took off toward the clubhouse. "You can have whatever balls are left."

Malik stood there, steaming. He'd found a gold mine, then shared it with his so-called friend. And how had Luis repaid him?

Well, never again, thought Malik. It was better to have no friends at all than friends like him. He headed back into the woods, blinking back bitter tears.

With Luis out of the picture, things started to go better. By four, Malik finally had a bagful of balls. But he still had to sell his collection in a hurry.

"Yo, mister!" he called, as the first foursome appeared at the fifteenth tee. "I got nice golf balls, a dollar a piece — but if you buy the whole mess of them, they're only fifty cents each!"

"How many you got there?" asked one of the men.

Malik had already counted. "Forty."

"Wow, forty. . . . I don't know. I don't need that many. How about you, Ned?"

"Nah, I've got enough."

"Why don't the four of you split 'em?" Malik suggested.

"Mmm . . ." The man named Ned looked around at his partners. "What say we get ten each?"

The men consulted, then agreed to go in on a purchase. Malik counted up his money — twenty dollars. Not a very good price for the day's work he'd put in, but he needed the money fast, so he could get back and buy the beautiful set of clubs.

He ran all the way to the subway, then waited on the platform for what seemed like hours. *Man, I could have walked home by now!* he thought, as the train finally rolled in.

He arrived at the garage sale at 5:05 P.M. He breathed a sigh of relief when he saw that the man was still there. He was boxing up what was left of his goods and throwing what he didn't want out onto the trash heap at the curb. Malik looked around for the clubs, but didn't see them.

"Oh, hey there!" the man greeted him with a sad smile. "You brought the money, did you?"

"Yup!" Malik said excitedly. "Fifty bucks, just like I said."

"Only thing is, you're about an hour too late," the man said with an apologetic shrug. "This other kid came by and offered me sixty bucks. Just about your age, too, except a little shorter."

"Did he say his name?" Malik asked, dreading the answer.

"Yeah . . . I forget it, though."

"Was it Luis?"

"Yeah, that's it! Luis. Cute little kid. You know him?"

"Yeah," Malik said, feeling a hard knot forming in his stomach. "I know him, all right."

9

That night, Malik couldn't sleep at all. His mom caught him raiding the fridge at two in the morning and asked him what was the matter.

"Can't sleep," Malik muttered.

"That much, I can see for myself," she said, sitting at the table in her nightgown and drumming her fingers. "So, what's on your mind?"

"Nuthin'," Malik said, not wanting to talk about it.

"Trouble at school?"

"No, Mama. I just can't sleep, that's all. Probably ate something bad."

"Like my cooking?"

"You know I like your cooking. Maybe something else."

"I notice Luis hasn't been by in a while. You two still tight?"

Malik hesitated. "Sure," he lied. "Sure we are."

"Uh-huh," his mom said. "I don't suppose this has anything to do with golf, does it?"

Malik stiffened. "Golf?"

"I was cleaning your closet the other day, and I couldn't help noticing . . ."

"Those clubs were Mr. Quigley's," he explained, in case she thought he'd stolen them or something.

"I see. I didn't know you were into golf."

"I'm not," he said. "Not anymore."

"No place to play around here anyway, is there?"

"There's a course on Eighty-sixth Street, and a driving range on Sixty-ninth."

"Really? I didn't know that," she said, smiling. "So you've been checking it out, huh?"

"Yeah, kind of," Malik admitted. "Anyway, I'm feeling tired now. Think I'll go to sleep."

"That's good," his mother said. "And you keep playing golf, Malik. I'd like for you to play a sport where you can't get hurt."

Malik didn't tell her about almost getting hit by golf balls, or about Luis's punches, which still hurt after two days. Truth was, it was his feelings that hurt the most — especially since he couldn't show them. Not even to his mom.

On Monday during lunch period, he cornered Luis. Malik put up his fists, ready for a showdown. "Yo, those clubs were mine," he told his ex-friend. "The guy was supposed to hold them for me."

"Yeah, well, he didn't, right? Too bad for you. I paid him ten bucks more than you were gonna, anyway."

"Cheating again, huh?" Malik said, knowing it would set Luis off.

Sure enough, Luis came at him, fists flying. Whistles blew, and the cafeteria erupted in cheers and yelling. Some kids rooted for Malik, some for Luis, but all of them were rooting for the fight to continue. They were disappointed when the cafeteria workers broke it up.

Luis's nose was bleeding, and Malik's ear was throbbing with pain. He knew he was going to have a bruise on his cheek, too. Lucky thing Luis had missed his eye. As it was, this was going to be tough to explain to his mother.

The two boys were brought to the principal's office at once. "I'm going to suspend you both if there's any more fighting," she said. "I would have done it this time, but Mr. Ridley tells me I should go easy on you."

Walking down the hall afterward, side by side, the boys were still steaming, not saying a word to each other. Then Malik broke the silence. "Yo, man — I know you bought those clubs just to get me. So how about I buy them from you for sixty-five dollars?"

"No way," Luis said, still holding a tissue to his nose. "Not now, not ever."

"Okay, seventy. Man, you're making money on the deal — and you know you're not gonna use those clubs."

"What makes you so sure?"

"Because you think it's for rich dweebs, and besides, you're not any good at it."

"Oh, so I should let the golf pro have the clubs, huh?"

"I'm not saying —"

"You're no better than I am. I beat you my first time out, remember?"

"Shut up, you did not!"

112

"Go ahead, hit me, fool," Luis dared him, knowing Malik didn't want to get suspended. Both boys knew that any suspensions would look really bad on their records — and Malik had a better record to spoil. Besides, his mama would have his sorry hide when she found out. "Go on. See what happens."

Malik broke away, heading for math class. "Who needs Luis, anyway?" he told himself. "He's a loser, and I'm better off without him." That's what he kept telling himself, even though he felt like he'd lost a brother.

Mr. Ridley made Malik stay after the final bell rang. "Thanks for talking to the principal," Malik said right off.

"You're welcome," Mr. Ridley replied. "Don't embarrass me by making me wrong."

"I won't," Malik promised. "But if Luis comes after me . . ."

"I'll speak to him — again," Mr. Ridley said. "Just don't provoke him."

"I won't."

"And, um, listen, Malik — I'm going to be driving some balls at the Sixty-ninth Street Pier this coming

Saturday. Want to join me? I could give you a few tips."

"You mean it?" Malik couldn't help smiling. Getting a free lesson from Mr. Ridley was even better than his plan to work for lessons from Al Sheinman! "What time?"

"How's eleven A.M.?"

"Cool — I'll be there!"

Whatever happened, Malik was going to get better at golf. If Luis was going to keep playing, one day there would be a challenge between them. Malik wanted to beat him in the worst way, but he would do it on the golf course — not with his fists, but with his game.

Malik showed up ten minutes early at the driving range that Saturday, but Mr. Ridley had beaten him there. "Glad to see you, Malik," he said, giving him a clap on the back. "Come on, get a club and let's go. And today's on me."

"Thanks, Mr. Ridley!" Malik said, relieved that he wouldn't have to spend any of this week's allowance on practice. That meant he could afford to play golf during the week without selling any used balls.

Mr. Ridley watched Malik hit a few shots, then started refining his grip. "You can interlock your fingers like this." He showed Malik. "That'll give you extra control. And line it up more off your front foot when you're driving, more off your back foot for shorter shots. That's it. Stand a little farther away, so you can extend your arms more."

Malik went through half a bucket of balls, then let Mr. Ridley hit a few. He had a long, graceful swing, and hit the ball a mile. Malik stood there, admiring the high arc of the shots.

Then, a movement to his left caught Malik's eye. He turned, and there was Luis.

"Hey, Mr. Ridley, here I am, ready to —" Luis stopped short, seeing Malik. "What the —?" he gasped, his smile vanishing.

"Hey!" Malik said, turning angrily to his teacher. "What's going on, Mr. Ridley?"

"Yeah," Luis echoed. "What is this? A trap? 'Cuz if it is, I'm outta here!"

"Me, too!" shouted Malik.

Just like that, a fun day had turned into Malik's worst nightmare!

10

Boys," Mr. Ridley said, "don't get upset now. I arranged things this way so we could get a few things straightened out, just the three of us, away from school and the other kids."

"I'm not talking to him," Luis said.

"Me neither!" Malik said. "I mean, I'm not talking to him either!"

Mr. Ridley sighed patiently. "Look, you two. I know you both like golf, and I know you like each other. So what's this really all about?"

Malik started to tell him all about how Luis had cheated, then stolen the golf set out from under him. Luis kept interrupting, calling Malik a liar, and saying *he* was the one who cheated.

"Hold on," Mr. Ridley said, holding up a hand. "It

sounds to me like you're more interested in competing with each other than getting better at golf *or* being friends. Is that true?"

"No," said Malik, looking down at the ground.

"*He's* the one who doesn't want to be friends," Luis said.

"Now, quit accusing," Mr. Ridley admonished him. "I'm sure Malik wants to be friends as much as you do. Don't you, Malik?"

Malik hesitated, then said, "Uh-huh," so softly he could barely be heard.

"There, you see?" Mr. Ridley said triumphantly. "And you both want to get better at golf, don't you?"

"Uh-huh."

"Yeah."

"Well, then, that's why I invited you both here today — separately. I knew neither of you would show up if he knew the other was coming. Plus, I figured it would be easier to give you both pointers together rather than separately. Besides," he added, "I've got a secret plan that involves the both of you — if you're willing to play along, that is."

"What is it?" Luis asked.

"Well," Mr. Ridley said, lowering his voice, "I've got this idea — Malik was the one who had it first, really — an idea to form a middle school golf team."

"Yes!" Malik said excitedly, practically jumping up and down.

"A golf team?" Luis asked, more cautious.

"Uh-huh. You'd both have to be on it, of course. I don't know if there are any other kids at school who even play. As cocaptains, you'd have to round up some more kids for the team."

"Cocaptains?" Luis and Malik repeated at the same time, looking at each other doubtfully.

"It's the only way," Mr. Ridley responded. "If one of you is captain and not the other — well, you can see why that wouldn't work. But if you're going to be cocaptains, you'll have to agree to work together. Question is, will you do it?"

"Cocaptains, huh?" Luis said, mulling it over. "I will if he will."

"Malik?"

Malik thought it over. "I don't know. He hates my guts."

"I don't think so," Mr. Ridley said softly. "Do you, Luis?"

"Not really," Luis said, kicking a nonexistent pebble. "I was just . . . I don't know . . . mad, I guess."

"Me, too," Malik said.

"Are you willing to shake hands and be cocaptains?" Mr. Ridley asked. "Because if you are, I'll go straight to the principal and ask her if we can go ahead with this."

"Okay," Malik said, offering his hand.

Luis took it. "Fine by me," he said, flashing a grin.

"We're on, then!" said Mr. Ridley, tousling their heads. "Let's go for it!"

The next few days flew by. Malik couldn't play golf, since he hadn't bothered to call ahead for a starting time. Oh, sure, he could have snuck on the course if it were a weekday — but on the weekends, the place was too crowded. And besides, Malik told himself, he was through with all that. No more cheating for him. He and Luis were going to build a team, and they were going to beat every other team, fair and square.

On Monday evening, Mr. Ridley called. Malik's mother answered, then handed him the phone, a puzzled, troubled look on her face. "You aren't failing math, are you?" she whispered as she handed Malik the phone.

"No, Ma, it's nothing like that," Malik assured her. "Wuzzup, Mr. Ridley?"

"Hey, Malik. Listen, I spoke to the principal today, and she's willing to let us try putting a team together."

"All right!"

"Well, wait now, it's not that simple. What she did was, she's allowing us to use athletic department funds to pay for you and Luis to get some practice rounds in before the end of the season."

"Excellent!" Malik said, getting more and more excited.

"Here's the catch, though. You and Luis have to convince four other kids to join the team by that time, or she won't enter us in the interschool league for the spring."

Malik was stunned. "But Mr. Ridley, how am I supposed to convince people to like golf?"

"You convinced Luis, didn't you?"

"Yeah, but, well, that was different. He's my friend."

"He's your only friend?"

"No, but, like, he's my best friend, see — so I

showed him how to make enough money to play. And I let him borrow my clubs."

"Well, I guess you and Luis will have to use some of those same tactics on the other kids."

"I guess." Malik hung up, feeling uncertain of himself. If he didn't succeed, his dream of a golf team would go up in smoke, just like that. This was his one chance. He couldn't afford to blow it.

The next morning, it was as if their fight had never happened. Now Malik and Luis were united in a common mission — identifying and recruiting the rest of their future golf team. Both boys stood outside the school before classes began, scouting other kids to see which of them would be likely candidates.

"We've gotta start with the coolest kid in the whole school," was Luis's opinion.

"That would be Oscar Romero," Malik said, stating the obvious. "Man, if we could get him on our team, everyone would want to be on it."

"I don't know," Luis said. "You're forgetting one thing — if Oscar said no, that would be the end of the whole team. If he said it wasn't cool, everyone would believe him."

"So how do we get him to say yes?"

The fact that he and Luis were even talking again was a miracle, Malik decided. So anything was possible. But Oscar Romero was cooler than cool. If he wore something one day, a dozen kids were wearing it the next. The week after that, half the school would be dressed that way — except Oscar wouldn't be one of them. He'd be on to the next cool thing, always blazing the trail for those who came after him.

"*You* go talk to him," Luis said. "You got me interested, right? So do the same thing with him."

"You're my friend," Malik reminded him.

"What, I'm not cool enough for you?"

"Cut it out, yo. You're cool, but not like Oscar. He doesn't even talk to me. Not much, anyway. *You* talk to him."

"Me? Forget it. You know more about golf. You talk to him."

"Tell you what, why don't we go together?"

"Okay, but you talk first."

"No, you."

"You."

They found Oscar Romero in the boys' room, combing his hair. "Golf?" he said, not believing his ears. "Are you for real? Talk to the hand, yo," he said, putting his palm out to indicate he didn't even want to hear it.

So much for Plan A. Luis and Malik put their heads back together, but all they could think of was to keep asking kids they thought of as cool, hoping at least one of them would say yes to being on the team.

It was hard going. Talking about golf, it just didn't sound that exciting. But both boys knew how much fun it was, once you got out on the course and started hitting the ball.

That didn't help them now, though. By Wednesday afternoon, they still hadn't found a single recruit. All they'd gotten was laughter and mockery. Malik and Luis were about ready to quit.

But not before their first weekly practice round with Mr. Ridley at Dyker. He met them after school, and they drove there in his car — a black SUV. They stopped first at each boy's house to load their clubs in the back, then headed for the course.

"So how's the search going?" Mr. Ridley asked them right off.

"Not so good, Mr. Ridley," Malik confessed.

"We've got nobody so far," Luis added for emphasis.

"Oh, I see. Well, keep trying. Maybe our round today will inspire you. I think what you guys need are some creative sales techniques."

"Huh?" Luis asked, puzzled.

"Later for that," Mr. Ridley said. "We're here. Let's get out on the course and play some golf!"

Mr. Ridley started in on them right away — correcting the way they "addressed" the ball, as he called it, adjusting their stance, their grip, their follow-through. They didn't keep score. If they hit the ball badly, they had to hit their next shot wherever it landed, just like in a real competition.

"Golf tournaments can work several ways," Mr. Ridley explained. "They can be medal play, which means they're scored the normal way — whoever gets the lowest score wins. Or they can be match play — each player against one from the other team, and whichever team wins the most matches wins. In the case of the interschool league, they play best ball."

"What's that?" asked Malik.

"Well, you've got a foursome — say, you two guys

versus two from the other team. Say you get a six on a hole, Malik, and Luis gets a four."

"Ha! I beat you!" Luis said. That angered Malik for a moment, until he saw that Luis was only joking.

"The two guys on the other team get fives," Mr. Ridley went on. "That's ten for each team, but because each team uses their best ball, you guys would win on Luis's four."

"Whew — it's complicated," Malik said.

"But it's fun, too, because it means you and Luis can root for each other, instead of playing against one another."

"That's cool," said Luis, and Malik thought he heard a note of relief in his friend's voice.

"We'll figure out handicaps for you, once we start our official practice rounds in April. Matches will be in May and June. That should give the team enough chances to practice between now and then — especially if we get some people on board quickly, so we can teach them before it gets too cold."

"Yeah," Luis said, "that's the thing, Mr. Ridley. Maybe *you* could get some kids to join, because we can't do it."

"Sure you can!" Mr. Ridley said, clapping them

both on the shoulder. Malik had felt like giving up just as much as Luis, but Mr. Ridley's enthusiasm was getting to him now, feeding him with good energy.

By the back nine, the boys were both hitting consistently good shots. "Next time, we keep score," Mr. Ridley said. "We'll try each week for lowest combined score, so you get used to being on the same side. The last thing we need is competition between our teammates before we go into the league."

"So how do we get kids to join?" Luis asked, bringing the conversation back around to the problem.

"Like I said — be creative."

"I don't get what you mean, Mr. Ridley," Luis said.

"Well, from what you're telling me, it's hard getting kids excited about golf, right?"

"Yeah," Malik said. "But if they ever played, they'd like it."

"So you've got to hook them with something else," Mr. Ridley said, his eyes dancing.

"You mean, like, a prize for trying golf?" Malik asked.

"There you go."

"Yo, I've got an idea!" Luis suddenly blurted out.

"I know this girl, Samaya — she paints T-shirts with this special paint? I could get some and do them up really cool, like with a golf logo."

"How 'bout a golf ball swoopin' through the air with a rainbow-colored trail behind it?" Malik suggested.

"Cool — and something jiggy written on the back, too!"

"I've got it," Malik said, slapping his hands together. "'Join the Club!' Get it? *The club?*"

"Yeah, man! And the ball could have the school's initials, and underneath, it could say, 'Golf Rocks!' Man, these shirts are gonna be phat — I oughta sell 'em for good money!"

"The idea," Mr. Ridley reminded him, "is to get the kids excited about it. But tell you what — I'll buy half a dozen T-shirts for you to experiment on, and some fabric paint, if you need it."

"We should wear the first two around as samples," Malik suggested.

"Yeah!" Luis said excitedly, giving their teacher a high-five. "Mr. Ridley, man — you rule! This is gonna work — I can feel it!"

11

While the T-shirts were being made, Malik busied himself thinking up other ways to get kids interested. He practiced and mastered a trick he'd seen a pro golfer do in a TV commercial, where he bounced a golf ball up and down on the head of an iron, over and over again. His little sister, Keisha, walked in on him practicing the trick and demanded to be taught how — so Malik decided it was something pretty cool.

He also dusted off his juggling skills. Pretty soon, he could juggle four golf balls in the air. He colored them different colors with indelible markers, and pretty soon, he was ready to rumble.

That Sunday, he went over to Luis's house to show him his mad new skills, and to see how the T-shirts were coming. "Man, these are phat!" he said, holding one of Luis's finished masterpieces. "I call this one."

"Nuh-uh," Luis said, grabbing it back from him. "That one's mine. You can have that one over there that's drying. It's cool, too. But this one was my first try, so I claim it."

On Monday, the two boys showed up at school with their hot new T-shirts. Luis went to find Mr. Ridley and give him his.

Then, at recess, Malik started doing his thing with the club and balls. Kids started gathering around, hooting and hollering and cheering him on:

"How do you do that, man?"

"Lemme try!"

"Cool beans!"

"We got a golf team now?"

By the end of that day, Malik had recruited two kids to come to the driving range with him. One of them was Curtis Ibanez, his and Luis's stickball buddy.

"Man, I'm gonna hit that ball so far they're never gonna find it!" Curtis was already bragging, strutting around in the T-shirt he'd put on.

Malik, watching him carry on, smiled to himself. He knew that you hit the ball farthest when your swing is in control, not when you try to kill the ball. Curtis had a lot to learn, and Malik couldn't wait to teach him.

Meanwhile, he was happy that a bunch of kids seemed interested in the whole team concept. He knew that the other stuff — getting good at the game by mastering your own weaknesses — would come later on, with lots of practice, just as it was coming along for him.

The next day, Malik was doing his recess thing again, when who should bop by but Oscar Romero — wearing one of Luis's T-shirts! Oscar was stylin', showing off for a half dozen girls who were giggling uncontrollably, blushing and acting like idiots to get Oscar's attention.

Soon, the whole school would be wearing golf team T-shirts, even if none of them ever lifted a club. It didn't matter, Malik thought. The money from the T-shirts would support those few who actually joined the team. The ball was rolling now, and nothing could stop it.

"Man," said Luis, shaking his head at his own phenomenal success. "I should have charged double and pocketed the change!"

Two weeks later, Mr. Ridley officially initiated the school's golf team. There were six of them now, enough to play matches with other schools when the season started in the spring. True, one of them was a girl — but hey, Malik thought, that was cool. At the driving range, Marissa had hit the ball farther than some of the guys. And Malik knew she could putt — he'd seen her at mini golf, knocking down holes in one.

"Okay, everyone," Mr. Ridley said, beaming as he looked at his team, dressed in their supercool T-shirts, just as he was himself. "Everybody please take these consent forms home and return them, signed by a parent. And I want you all to know that we've raised enough money for practice rounds, and to purchase four used sets of clubs for the team!"

A huge cheer went up from the kids, including Malik. Sure, his set would probably be the worst of them all, but he didn't care. It was so cool to have a bunch of kids he knew, playing on a golf team with him.

Next spring was going to be a blast, thought Malik — and so was next summer, because Mr. Ridley had offered him and Luis jobs as caddies at his club in Staten Island!

Malik was totally golf-crazy now, and he promised himself he wouldn't stop playing and practicing until he was the best golfer he could be.

The only problem now was, *How was he going to get through the winter?*

Matt Christopher®

Muhammad Ali

Lance Armstrong

Kobe Bryant

Jennifer Capriati

Jeff Gordon

Ken Griffey Jr.

Mia Hamm

Tony Hawk

Ichiro

Derek Jeter

Randy Johnson

Michael Jordan

Mario Lemieux

Tara Lipinski

Mark McGwire

Yao Ming

Shaquille O'Neal

Alex Rodriguez

Babe Ruth

Curt Schilling

Sammy Sosa

Venus and Serena Williams

Tiger Woods

The #1 Sports Series for Kids

Read them all!

*Previously published as Crackerjack Halfback

Lacrosse Face-Off

Line Drive to Short **

Long-Arm Quarterback

Long Shot for Paul

Look Who's Playing First Base

Miracle at the Plate

Mountain Bike Mania

No Arm in Left Field

Nothin' But Net

Penalty Shot

Prime-Time Pitcher

Red-Hot Hightops

The Reluctant Pitcher

Return of the Home Run Kid

Roller Hockey Radicals

Run For It

Shoot for the Hoop

Shortstop from Tokyo

Skateboard Renegade

Skateboard Tough

Slam Dunk

Snowboard Champ

Snowboard Maverick

Snowboard Showdown

Soccer Duel

Soccer Halfback

Soccer Scoop

Stealing Home

The Submarine Pitch

The Team That Couldn't Lose

Tennis Ace

Tight End

Top Wing

Touchdown for Tommy

Tough to Tackle

Wheel Wizards

Windmill Windup

Wingman on Ice

The Year Mom Won the Pennant

**Previously published as Pressure Play   All available in paperback from Little, Brown and Company